For Those Who Need Help To Feel

Book 3 of The Three Shots Series

Jannah Jette

For Those Who Need Help

To Feel

Book 3 of

The Three Shots Series

ISBN: 979-8-9998104-7-2

No part of this book was written or illustrated using AI.

Table of Contents

Dedication

Since my editor didn't write one for me this time, I suppose I will. This book is for all of my flawed readers. My chronic illness readers. My battling addiction readers. My happy or sad readers. I hope you find a connection to someone in here…so long as it's not one very specific person. If you connect with that person, just turn yourself into the cops.

Now.

Content Warning

For Those Who Need Help To Feel contains content that could be triggering to some. This includes, but is not limited to-

Being assaulted

Being drugged

Rape

Death

Graphic Consensual Sex Scenes

Prologue

Six Years Ago

"Dude, Reed. I met the hottest girl today. Anyway, if you have plans tonight, you have to cancel them. I guess her friend, Gina, just moved to town, and she is refusing to go on a date with me unless it is a double date. I offered to take them both out and then home, but Jessa declined that offer."

Reed looks down at the paperwork in front of him. "I kind of have a lot to get done here, man. Another night."

I lean over his desk and put a brown folder on top of one of the many stacks. "Let's just hide this one, and now you have less to get done tonight. Come on, Reed. I need you. If you combined Jessica Alba with Amanda Peet but made her a ginger, you would have Jessa. I can't switch nights. This is a once-in-a-lifetime kind of girl!"

Reed huffs out, "Fine, but you owe me big time for agreeing to this, and I plan to sit there silently the whole night. I will make the entire date so awkward on purpose."

I shrug. "Do it. I don't care how you act. I just need your body there. Your only goal is to make sure that this Gina chick has someone to sit by so I can work my magic."

Reed wipes his hand down his face. "I already know that I am going to regret this."

******

Five Years Ago

"I am telling you, Reed, there is something about her. I can't put my finger on it, but my eyes can see the red flags waving all around her. I think you need to tap the brakes because I just have this really bad feeling."

Reed shakes his head. "Or you can quit being your dramatic self. Gina has no red flags. I don't know why you would even think that."

"Like I said, I can't put my finger on it, but my gut is telling me that something is off, and you know my gut is always right. Always!"

Reed leans across the table. "Brad, I am asking her to marry me tonight. Maybe you are just scared of losing me. I mean, I would be scared if I were you."

I scoff. "Why would I be scared of losing you?"

Reed grins. "Because Gina is way prettier than you are."

"I have no fear. I am irreplaceable," I laugh out.

Reed shakes his head with a chuckle. "That you are, my friend. That you are."

******

Four Years Ago

"Please do not punch me when I say this, but when that baby is born, you really should get a DNA test done."

Reed glares at me. "Don't start again, Brad."

I throw my hands in the air. "Reed, I swear to you that I saw her leaving that hotel with Dumb Fuck Daniel from your office. Obviously, I don't know what happened in the hotel, but why else would she be meeting him there?"

Reed rolls his eyes. "I am getting extremely tired of this conversation, Brad."

I shake my head in defeat. "Okay, man. I will drop it."

******

Three Years Ago

"I do not understand why you put up with this from her."

Reed switches Lola to his other arm and puts the empty bottle on the coffee table. "She is my wife, Brad. She is the mother of my daughter. She is dealing with postpartum, and I need to give her some grace."

I stand from the couch and begin pacing the living room floor. "If she were actively seeing a doctor and receiving treatment, I could buy that excuse. Her going out drinking every other night with "clients" while you are at home with the baby seems a little more than just postpartum depression."

Reed stands to sway Lola to sleep. "I think if you read about it, you would find that this is a coping mechanism for her. It will ease up. I just have to give her time."

I stop my pacing and face Reed. "And you are fine watching her treat you, James, Betty, and Lola with all of this disrespect? Because I am definitely not, Reed. You can blame whatever you want, but I have been telling you for years that something has felt off with her. Last night should have been a flashing neon light that read, 'Told you so.' Are you going to let that just get swept under the rug, too?"

Reed turns to take a sleeping Lola upstairs to her crib. "Last night was an accident."

Following him, I scoff. "Who throws a lit candle at an elderly lady while she is holding a baby, Reed? She could have hurt both of them. And for what?"

Reed shakes his head. "She was mad at me, and Betty walked in at the wrong time."

"For what, Reed? Say it out loud so you can hear how asinine it is."

Reed turns to me sharply. "Enough, Brad."

I shake my head. "Fucking say it!"

Reed lets out a sigh. "Because I wouldn't have sex with her while she was drunk."

I put my hands out, palms up. "Does that warrant throwing a lit candle at the woman who practically raised you while she was holding your infant daughter?"

Reed runs his hand down his face. "No, Brad. I know this. She agreed that she would get help. I am trying. I really am. I can't take any more of this conversation today."

I shake my head and walk out of Lola's bedroom.

******

Two Years Ago

"I really think you should consider putting a restraining order against her."

Reed walks into the kitchen with the baby monitor in his good hand. "She agreed to get the divorce; no point in getting a restraining order now. She hired movers, they will be here by the end of the week to start moving her things."

I open the fridge to grab a beer. "She assaulted you and broke your wrist, Reed. You need to file charges."

"I told the hospital that the hammer fell from an old, rickety shelf that broke. That is the story I am sticking to."

I shake my head in disbelief. "What the fuck, man. Why are you refusing to hold her accountable?"

Reed snaps towards me. "Someday, you will understand, Brad. Someday, someone will come along who changes you so completely that you will forgive them for their mistakes because your love for them is so strong that you can see the good in them, even behind the bad moments or situations. You will forgive their lapses in judgment because you know that deep down, that lapse comes from a place of hurt or vulnerability. Not because they are a bad person. Someday."

"You don't know me then, Reed. Even after three decades of friendship. I will never allow someone to treat me this way and forgive them."

Reed leans against the counter. "We will see about that when the time comes, won't we?"

******

One Year Ago

"I can't wait for the day that Lola turns eighteen and none of us have to deal with Gina again."

Reed smacks the back of my head. "Keep your voice down! I don't want Lola to hear us talking negatively about her mother. That would ruin all of the progress we have made in co-parenting."

I rub the back of my head. "I still mean what I said. I do not understand how you are so calm about everything. This is the fifth weekend in a row that she has cancelled on Lola. The fifth weekend in a row that I had to watch my niece walk up the stairs with tears in her eyes after you told her that, once again, her mother was not coming to get her. What in this entire world could be more important than Lola? Answer me that, Reed. What?"

Reed shakes his head and drops his voice to a whisper, "I am not saying that I don't agree with you. It is killing me, too. But I can't change the situation, I can only control how I handle it. So, we are going to pretend nothing is wrong, we are going to go get Lola, and then we are going to go to that place she likes to eat with the cornhole game. You are going to let her whoop your ass, and we will try to salvage the night."

I nod. "Yeah, let's do that. But I still think you need to have a serious conversation with Gina about this. She can't keep doing this to her. For years, you have let her get away with everything. You need to put your foot down, Reed."

Reed waves a hand in the air. "I will talk to her. Not today. But I will talk to her. Now, who is going to get our Princess?"

I start walking towards the stairs. "I will, I need the distraction before I call her myself."

******

Present Day

"Chris just called. Lola still isn't talking, but it doesn't sound like she saw anything from Peter's windows. Avery said she kept her on the other side of the house. Chris is taking her over to her house until we leave here. Reed? Did you hear me?"

Reed stares at the door blankly but nods his head.

"Okay, Avery is back upstairs with James and said she would stay with him tonight. The detectives got what they needed from you. Just waiting for the doctor to discharge you now. Where do you want to stay tonight? Do you and Lola want to stay at my house? Want me to find a hotel?"

Reed continues to stare blankly at the door.

I crouch down in front of his face. "Reed. I know today was traumatic, but we have to pull ourselves together for Lola. Tell me where you want to stay tonight, and I will be there to take care of her so you can have time to process things privately. But you have to at least point me in the right direction."

Reed shifts his eyes to me. "I don't know what to do. Don't let me pick. Obviously, I don't make good decisions, Brad."

I clap his shoulders and pull him into a hug. "Okay. You two will be staying with me. I'm going to step out and make a quick phone call. Okay?"

Reed just nods and shifts his gaze back to the invisible spot on the door.

I walk out of the hospital and to my truck as casually as I can. I am praying that the bottle of whiskey Avery and I bought a few weeks ago is still in here. At the time, hiding it under the backseat from Sandy seemed like a good idea. It was Halloween night, and she was a mess from jail. Avery and I wanted to hide the crutch we used to calm ourselves over that whole situation. Watching Sandy hobble around was hard enough; seeing the bruising with the hobble made it nearly unbearable to watch. The whiskey was a quick fix to relax our tempers. If we knew then what we know now, I wouldn't have hidden anything. I wouldn't have numbed the pain or the anger. I would have let it rage!

Flipping over a duffel bag with old books to donate in it, I find the small bottle of whiskey. Just enough left in the bottle for two good swigs. I open it and desperately down the contents of it. Anything to get a little bit of the numbing I need to be the rock that Reed and Lola need me to be now. Or at least enough to fake being the rock for them. I can do that.

Chapter 1
Brad

Nearly three months later

"Happy Valentine's Day, Brad."

I turn to my left to see the blonde barfly who is at this bar just as much as I am, if not more. I dig through my brain to try to remember her name, and not just her atrocious nickname we call her. *Back alley… Back alley… Shit… Back-alley Becky? Close, but no. Back-alley Bree. That's it. Easy, sleezy, breezy.* "Happy Valentine's Day, Bree."

Her salacious smile and grazing of my arm turn my dick into an innie. Even if she hadn't sucked off nearly every guy that has ever stepped foot in this place, I can't look at a blonde without being reminded of Sandy anymore. Even when I spend nearly every night in this run-down, hole-in-the-wall bar, drinking to forget her and the tragedy that I didn't stop from happening. This barstool has become my lifeline. The only time I feel something other than numb is when I am sitting on my neon, backlit throne.

"Brad, same old same old?" Patsy asks me from behind the bar.

I give her my most innocent smile. "You know it, Patsy Fine."

Patsy rolls her eyes. "Why did you have to pick the worst nickname to cling to?

My grin grows wider. "Because I'm crazy for loving you," I sing to her.

She swats me with a bar towel and shuffles around behind the bar fixing my order.

I take this time to glance around. Mack is setting up for karaoke. A small group of college girls are crowding around the karaoke book and giggling. "Ten dollars says they sing Spice Girls," I whisper to myself.

"Twenty says they sing TLC."

I turn to my left, where the counter bet just came from. A gorgeous, petite woman with long, jet black hair, tanned skin, and the clearest and lightest green eyes I have ever seen smirks at me.

I pull my hand to my chin. "Hmmm, I will take that bet." I throw my hand out to the little vixen beside me as Patsy puts my three shot glasses in front of me.

The vixen shakes my hand and then points to my three shots. "Partying hard tonight?"

I shake my head. "Undecided," I say, glancing over at her. "This is a toast. Care to join me?"

The vixen eyes the shots carefully and shrugs. "Why not?"

I wave a hand over my drinks. "My sweet and sultry, Patsy Fine. Will you get a setup for my new friend… uh… what is your name?"

The vixen smiles. "Quinn."

I wave over the glasses again. "Will you get a setup for my new friend, Quinn, please?"

Patsy starts rummaging around for shot glasses, and I turn to face the vixen. "Quinn? Unique name."

Quinn smirks. "Thanks. It was a gift. First one I received on my birthday."

Feisty. I smirk back. "And the second was that sassy ass mouth of yours."

She cocks her head to the side. "No, that was the third gift."

"And what was the second then?" I ask.

She looks straight into my eyes. "The wit to supply the sassy ass mouth."

I stand from my barstool and drop to one knee. Grabbing Quinn's left hand, I beg, "Will you marry me now or make me woo you? I can wait if I need to, but you just stole my heart with your sexy, sassy ass mouth."

"Don't say yes, sweetie. He asked me to marry him just last night," Patsy says in her raspy voice.

I stand. "Damnit, Pats. You declined, so it doesn't count." I fall to my barstool with a huff, but glance to see that Quinn is smiling. Not a smirk or a forced, polite smile. A genuine ear-to-ear smile. It is stunning.

"Alright, Casanova. Teach me your toast," she says, pointing to the shots that are now in front of her.

I grab a shot and encourage her to do as I do. She grabs one and watches me attentively. I clink our shot glasses. "For those who hurt." I tip my shot back and she does the same. I clink our second round of shot glasses. "For those who heal." We both down our shots. I stare directly into her eyes as I clink our third shot. "For those who need help to feel."

With the slam of our final shot, she looks at me and wipes her mouth with the back of her hand. "Sorrowfully poetic. I like it."

"Welcome out to Nightengale's Roost, where all our songbirds congregate and others come to copulate. Just kidding. Don't copulate in the bar. Save that for the cab ride home. Not kidding. If you drink irresponsibly, take a cab. Don't drink and drive, folks. I want to see you back here next week. I'm Mack, and I will be your KJ for the night.

Don't be shy, let my songbirds fly. Come sign up for a song or five."

I turn to Quinn and tap her knee with my own. "You should put that wit to use and write him a new script. That one is getting old."

Quinn shrugs and pats my thigh. "I'll consider it."

Mack queues up the song he plays while plugging in the chosen karaoke song, and the gaggle of giggling girls run up to the stage. One of the girls has her hand cupped over her brow so she can see through the light into the crowd, like she is looking for someone. Spotting her target, she waves in the direction of where I am sitting.

Quinn takes a sip from the beer Patsy placed in front of her before standing. "That's my cue. I'll collect my twenty when I get back. Watch my drink for me, Nova."

I stare in awe as Quinn and this group of college girls sing the worst rendition of "No Scrubs" I have ever heard. Even Avery can carry a tune in comparison. They are all dancing around and having the time of their life up there, and it hits me deep in a spot that is not allowed at this bar. This bar is one of my reprieve destinations. I turn and wave down Patsy, silently asking for a whiskey on the rocks. Once the drink is in front of me, I focus on that and that drink alone.

"Sad over losing a Jackson from your wallet?" Quinn asks as she sits back down on the barstool to my right.

I offer her a quick glance before downing the whiskey in front of me. "Nope. Least of my concerns." I grab my wallet, slap a twenty in front of Quinn and a fifty down for Patsy. "Have a safe night, Quinn."

One of the regulars, Ron, is walking up to sing. Normally, I like to watch him. The man should be on Broadway but wastes his talent on the people in this bar that don't appreciate his ability to belt out every song from Les Misérables. Patsy walks over to grab the money I put down for her while I grab my coat from the back of the barstool.

Quinn reaches out and places a hand on my bicep. "What's your name?"

"Nova. Right?" I ask as I slip on my coat.

Quinn bites her bottom lip. "Oh. Got it. Well then, have a nice night, Nova. Or the night you deserve, I suppose," she says bluntly before turning away from me.

Without even thinking, I reach out and spin her barstool around. That phrase triggering hurt inside me. "What did you say?"

Quinn stares at me with wide eyes.

"What. Did. You. Say?"

Quinn stands. She only comes up to mid chest on me. With her hands now on her hips, head tilted back to stare into my eyes, she says, "I said have a nice night, Nova. Or the night you deserve."

I feel my chest tightening. "Why would you say that to me?"

She waves her hand between us. "You decided to brush me off after asking for my hand in marriage. Don't even have the decency to tell me your real name. So, Nova, I don't know if you deserve to have a nice night, therefore I amended my original nicety." She pokes her finger into my chest. "So, have the night you deserve."

I watch as she grabs a jacket off her barstool and stomps out of the bar. I look at Patsy, "Does she have an open tab?"

Patsy shakes her head. "Nope. She paid cash with her order." Patsy cocks her head toward the door. "Go make sure she's okay, will ya? She's a friend of the family. Make sure no one bothers her in the parking lot for me, sugar."

I nod and head to the front door. The cold air sends a shock through me at first. I glance around to see if I can find a car's interior lights on. She wouldn't have had enough time to get in and leave already. I walk towards the side of the building and find Quinn leaning against it with her phone in her hand, not even realizing that she is not alone.

"You should pay closer attention to your surroundings," I say.

Quinn jumps, clutching her chest. "Jesus! What is wrong with you? You don't sneak up on women like that!"

I place my palms in the air. "I just came to check on you. Make sure you got to your car safely."

She pulls her phone back up. "I didn't drive tonight; I'm just waiting on my Uber. You can go and act like a prick somewhere else now."

I dip my head to make her look at me. "Whoa. I am sorry if you felt my mood was directed at you. It wasn't. It is all me and my own head. I never meant to be rude to you in any way."

She looks up at me and gives me a single nod, acknowledging that she heard me and that she doesn't believe me.

I place my hands on either side of her face and bring her eyes back to mine. "You are the only thing that has brought me genuine laughter in a long while. I am sorry that my mood affected your night. How can I make it up to you?"

She stares at me quizzically for a few minutes before responding, "I need another drink but with less singing."

I grab her hand. "I know just the place," I say as I lead her towards my truck.

Chapter 2
Brad

I drive us to an even more dingy bar a few blocks over from the Nightengale's Roost. This building is tiny, with tape holding up panels on the wall in some places, and it rarely has more than a handful of people in it. I wave to the bartender, Frank, and lead Quinn to the far side of the bar, where there is a small, secluded, rounded booth.

"Bring all your dates here?" Quinn asks, taking in the run-down bar.

I side-eye her. "Is this a date now?"

Quinn shrugs. "Well, I would expect so if you plan to be my *potential* future husband."

I lean back in the booth. "I see. What do you want to drink, my *potential* future wife? I will go get us a round while I figure out my game plan here."

"Any light beer will do," she says, looking up at me.

I lean over and place a kiss on her cheek. "Anything for my *potentia*l fiancé."

I watch the blush that takes over her cheeks and enjoy that view for a second before standing and walking up to the bar. "Frank, good to see you. I'll have my usual and whatever light beer you have that's the coldest."

Frank grumbles, "All my beer is cold. The coldest in town."

I chuckle. "If you say so, Frank." I glance around and see there are only three older gentlemen here tonight. I lean over the bar so only Frank can hear me when I ask, "Hey, will you let me play DJ tonight?"

Frank looks towards the booth and then back at me. "To make that lass smile?"

I nod.

Frank hits some buttons on the cash register. "$18.50 for the drinks, add a twenty on top of that, and I will give you two hours of playing DJ without me rejecting anything."

I slap down a fifty. "Deal!"

I run over to the juke box, feed it two twenties and start making my selections. I have to be methodical about my song selections. Once I am satisfied with my music choices, I grab our drinks off the bar top and make my way back to the booth. Quinn finishes typing out a text and drops her phone into her lap.

"Took you a while. Did it take that long to come up with a plan?"

I really like her sass. "No, that juke box is just slow. Now, scoot over so our date can officially start."

We spent the next forty-five minutes asking ridiculous questions, telling embarrassing stories, laughing with and at each other while Frank kept the drinks coming. The old man even brought them to our table rather than making us walk to the bar. I know he will charge me extra for that, but I don't mind. Getting to watch Quinn's face light up and that cute scrunch of her nose when she laughs is worth every penny I own.

"You still haven't told me your name. I am beginning to worry that I made a grave mistake and maybe you are some serial killer with some bartender accomplices or something," Quinn says, glancing up at me.

I glance down at her beside me. "My name is Brad. Brad Bennet."

Quinn smirks. "Hmmmm, Bennet. Quinn Bennet." Her green eyes find mine, and she blushes. "Unfortunately, that doesn't sound awful together, so I will have to find another reason to refuse your offer for an engagement by the end of the night."

I grab her chin lightly and lean in close to her. My lips are so close that I can feel her breath hitting them.

Glancing from eye to eye, I softly say, "My dancing will give you the escape route you need. Come on, let me show you."

Right on time, as I had planned, a slow melody plays from the juke box. I grab her hand and pull her out of the booth to a spot between tables that gives us a few feet of room to dance around. The slow country song starts us off with a nice sway. One of her legs between mine, one of her arms wrapped around my lower back, her head rests against the middle of my chest, while her other hand lies softly in mine. I hum along as I lead us around a few tables before bringing us back to the little section where the tables are a little more widespread again. Our dance floor for the night.

The second song starts, and she goes to pull her head back from my chest. I run my hands from her shoulders, up to the back of her neck, where it meets her hair and push her head back into my chest.

"Where do you think you are going, Quinnie? You haven't even gotten to experience all my dance moves yet. I have moves you've never even seen before. This is the warmup," I say to her.

She looks up at me. "I don't know if I am concerned or excited."

I let out a low chuckle. "Just enjoy the ride."

She lays her head back against my chest, and I let my hand roam the length of her neck for the rest of the song. Each song is progressively picking up the tempo. By the time Spice Girls come on, Quinn and I are both swaying and jumping around, singing along to the songs. Sex Is On Fire plays and Quinn is standing in front of me with her back to my chest, swinging her hips and grinding against me. Her hair is a wild mess from shaking her head side to side with the beat. My hands fall to her hips, gripping her, feeling the energy radiating off of her. She turns around, and it is as if time has stopped. The music is gone, the few other people in the bar disappeared, and it is just me and her. Her hands snake up my chest, hips still swaying, as she links her hands behind my neck. She raises her head to stare up at me, pulls my head down to hers, and plants her full lips against mine.

Our kiss went from cautious to desperate in a matter of seconds. One second, we are simply touching lips, letting them mingle. The next, my hands are fisting the oversized sweater she is wearing as I tug her body impossibly closer to mine. Her tongue is invading my mouth, and I am all for it. She has one hand gripping my hair and the other gripping my shoulder to help her keep her balance on her tiptoes. I lead her off our makeshift dance floor and back to our private booth. I sit on the edge of the seat, while she stands over my legs, running her hand through my hair.

"Brad Bennet, you will ruin me. One way or another. I just know it," she says before leaning forward and kissing me softly again.

I pull back just far enough to whisper against her lips, "Quinnie, you are safe with me."

She studies me for a second before I pull her lips back to mine. Her lips breathing life back into me. Like my lungs haven't had air since November. My heart hadn't made a full beat. Like this little woman in front of me has shocked all of my organs back to life.

She takes a step back. "I am going to run to the ladies' room. Want to get us another round? Maybe another shot as well?"

I nod and ask, "Yeah, shot preference?"

She shrugs. "Anything but Jager. Too many bad nights with that."

"Gotcha. Go do your thing," I say with a smack to her perfect bubble butt. Levi's were made for her, and she wears them well.

She brings her hands up to her lips and turns to walk to the bathroom but stops short and turns back to me.

With a shake of her head, she resumes her course towards the bathrooms.

I walk up to the bar and find Frank waggling his eyebrows as I approach.

"I have never seen you show any interest in a single woman in months, and then tonight you show up here with the prettiest woman that ever stepped foot inside my bar. What gives?" Frank asks while collecting our next round of drinks.

"Apparently, Cupid. That would be the only thing to explain any woman that gorgeous even giving me the time of day," I say.

Frank shakes his head. "You are too hard on yourself, Brad."

I am ready to list the reasons that I am not when a hand lands on mine. I glance to the left and see it is not my little Quinnie. "Tiffany, how lovely to see you," I say as I pull my hand away from hers.

"Same. I thought you said you weren't coming out tonight. Something about Valentine's Day being a bullshit holiday or something?" She leans in closer, and I can smell the cheap booze on her breath. "Did you change your plans after I asked you to meet me here to be my Valentine?"

Chapter 3
Quinn

I walk out of the bathroom but stop in the doorway when I see a dirty blonde-haired woman talking to Brad. Thanks to the alcohol running through me, my initial reaction wants to slap him, and believe that he came here to see her, but the logical side of my brain remembers that I asked him to take me somewhere quieter. But he was standing to leave. Maybe he was about to head here regardless. Then why would he have brought me along?

I reevaluate his stance. He visibly looks uncomfortable, even from behind. Rigid stance, hands behind his back, keeps looking over to Frank to avoid looking at this woman. The alcohol induced part of my brain takes over again.

I walk up behind Brad and place a hand on his lower back, sliding my hand with me as I walk around the front of him, lift my arms to his shoulders, and jump up to wrap my legs around his waist. Like we are of one mind, he grips my ass, holding me in place.

"Pookie, I think I am ready to go home for the night." I turn to face the woman who I pretended not to notice before. "Oh, Pooks, I am so sorry. Were you in the middle of something?" I ask Brad, trying to force a sincerely apologetic look on my face.

Brad kisses my neck. "No, my little Jellyfish. I was just waiting on you when Tiffany here walked up to wish us a happy Valentine's Day."

I twist my torso to face Tiffany a little better, putting my barely more than ample right breast so close to Brad's face that I can feel his breath through my sweater. "Oh, that is so sweet. Happy Valentine's Day to you too, Tiffany." I turn my torso back to Brad and run my fingers through his hair while looking down into his eyes. "I think I am ready to call it a night, Pooks. Can we go home now? Please?"

Brad looks from my eyes to Frank and then back to me. "Frank, give those to whoever wants them. We settled?"

Frank groans. "Yeah, for now."

Brad, still looking deep into my eyes, says, "Good. My jellyfish wants to go home."

Brad turns and begins to walk out of the bar with me still in his arms. I look over his shoulder and leave Tiffany with a condescending southern style wave before shooting Frank a wink with a smile. Brad doesn't put me down until we are at his truck and when he does, it is reluctantly.

"That was brilliant," he says as he runs a hand through my hair at the base of my neck. He shakes his head. "No one, and I mean no one has ever put on a show with me like that. Did you take improv classes in school?"

I tip my head back further to look at him. "No, just played the pretend girlfriend for a lot of my gay friends who weren't ready to open the closet door yet in high school."

Brad drops his forehead to mine. "You were spectacular. Though we should work on your nicknames."

I bring my hand to my chest like I am offended. "Mine? Yours! Jellyfish?"

Brad leans down further and brings his mouth so close to my ear that I can feel his breath as he says, "You are mesmerizing to look at, able to adapt to your surroundings with fluidity, you are resilient, and bring this peaceful feeling. But when you wrapped your legs around me, I knew that you are going to cause me to feel so many sensations that I won't realize the pain you leave me with until it's too late."

Brad pulls back and looks down at me. I stare up at him with my mouth open, unable to form words. So, I don't. I grab his shirt and pull him down to me for a desperate kiss. His hands go straight for my hips, and he lifts me up. I wrap my legs around him and we stay like this. Making out like horny teenagers in a bar parking lot long enough that I hear at least eight different muffled songs from inside before the music stops.

Brad chuckles against my lips. "My two hours are up."

I look at him quizzically.

"I had to pay Frank extra to let me take over the juke box for two hours. That was the last song that I had picked that just finished."

I cock my head to the side. "You paid the bartender to let you pay to play music when you could have just paid to play the music?

Brad frowns. "Well, when you put it like that, yeah, it sounds silly. But you see, there was this extremely gorgeous woman that I was trying to please, and for whatever reason, she wanted to spend her time with me tonight, so I wasn't necessarily thinking straight."

I shake my head but can't shake the ear-to-ear grin that is plastered on my face. I playfully smack Brad's shoulder. "Alright, Pookie. Put me down. I should get an Uber; it is getting pretty late."

Brad slowly lowers me to the ground but doesn't remove his hands from my hips. "I will take you wherever you want to go."

I shake my head. "Honestly, we probably both need an Uber or a cab at this point. We did a lot of shots in there."

Brad nods his head. "You are probably right. I have the cab's number saved in my phone. I'll get us one." Brad walks to the back of his truck, lowers the tailgate, and lifts me on to it before walking around to the passenger side. A couple of seconds later, he returns with a couple oversized throw blankets. "While I call, fold one of these up for a cushion for our asses and then we will cover up with the other. I don't need you catching a cold while we wait."

I begin folding one into a cushion while he gives the cab company the address of the bar and where to find us. Not that you can't easily find us here. There are only seven cars in the entire parking lot. When he is done, he jumps up into the bed of the truck, pulls the blanket cushion to the back, sits on it, and leans against the back of the truck. He spreads his legs and pats the cushion in between his thighs for me to come sit there. With the other blanket in my hand, I follow his silent order and cover us once I am settled. His large arms wrap around me under the blanket.

"So, Jelly, how shall we pass our time? We have roughly a half hour before the cab will arrive."

I lean my head back against his broad chest. "Tell me something interesting about you that no one else knows."

"No one or nearly no one?"

"Not a single soul."

His chest expands with the deep breath he takes. "That is a tough one. I am a pretty open book. Give me an easier one while I consider that question in the back of my mind."

I shake my head. "Don't think that you are getting out of answering that one."

He chuckles softly. "I wouldn't dream of it."

I run my fingers over the back of his hands and stare at the stars like they will give me the questions to ask. "What did you want to be as a kid compared to what you became as an adult?"

"Easy! I wanted to be a member of a boy band, but I suck at singing. You know how the saying goes. Those who can, do."

I giggle. "Those who can't, teach."

He kisses the back of my head. "Precisely. I am a music teacher. Then, during the summer, I volunteer at a farm that a friend's mom owns, provide music lessons to the less fortunate in surrounding communities, volunteer to play piano for the kid's theater here and there, or I spend the time with my niece."

I look over my shoulder at Brad. "Are you fucking kidding me?"

Brad looks at me incredulously. "Why would I kid about that?"

I shake my head. "How is it that I go out and run into the one last decent guy in the entire state of Florida? I am not that lucky. I mean, you volunteer at a farm and teach kids how to play music."

"Don't forget the part about playing for their theater."

I lightly smack my forehead. "How could I forget that."

"I don't know. That's my best quality. What about you?"

I lean my head against his shoulder so I can tilt my head towards his a little bit. "I wanted to be a zookeeper but am in my last month of the accelerated Bachelor of Science in Nursing program. I debated going to be a Registered Nurse but decided to put in the extra effort for this instead."

Brad leans his head against mine. "Hmmm, overachiever. You are either an only child or the middle child."

I let out a soft laugh. "Only. You?"

"Middle. I have an older and younger sister. Why else would being in a boy band have been my childhood dream job?"

I shrug. "Hip parents?"

He chuckles. "No, my dad was a principal, and my mom was a manager at a retail store that primarily sold Christian based merchandise. The first time they saw me rolling my hips while singing a song, my mom nearly fainted and my dad told me to go to the library and read about the 'good' musicians. It made me fall in love with all things music…so, I guess they did help me, in a weird way."

"I think you turned out alright."

He kisses the back of my head again. "Thank you, Jelly."

I notice headlights pulling into the bar parking lot and look up to see two cabs.

"Ah, your chariot, my dear," Brad says.

I stand and walk to the edge of the truck bed. "You called for two cabs?"

Brad rolls the blankets, walks to the tailgate, and jumps down. Lifting his arms up to me he says, "Yes. I told you that you are safe with me. There is no denying our chemistry, and it would be too easy for us to make decisions tonight that would be better made sober. So, I got us each our own cab."

I walk into his open hands and let him help me down from the truck. Once I am on solid ground, I grab one side of his shirt and pull his cheek down to me before kissing it. "You are the last of the true gentleman, Pookie."

He walks me over to my cab, opens the door, and then closes it behind me once I am in. I watch him walk around the front and give the cab driver a hundred-dollar bill before coming back and tapping on my window for me to roll it down.

I crack it open. "Can I help you?"

He looks through the crack. "Are you going to give me your number so that I can give you my answer to the first question?"

I shake my head. "No. I am not."

He cocks his head to the side.

"If I give you my number now, we will talk for a bit, have our fun, and fizzle out. If you are meant to be in my life, we will cross paths again. Tell me then." With that, I roll up my window and whisper yell for my cab driver to go so that I can't change my mind. I know my luck and the type of guys that end up in my orbit. They all seem great at first, but they always burn me. If it is meant to be, it will be. God, do I hope he is meant to be.

Chapter 4
Brad

"You were out late last night," Reed says before passing me my coffee.

"Yeah. Interesting night," I say nonchalantly.

"Are you going to elaborate?" Reed asks.

"Not yet. I don't know if I will ever see her again. She wouldn't give me her number and wants to leave it to fate. So, if the day comes, I will tell you about it."

Reed shrugs. "Okay."

Lola walks out of the room she has been staying in at my house while their new house is being built. I don't blame either one of them for never wanting to step foot back in the house where Gina killed Sandy before turning the gun and ending her own life as well. Lola still hasn't said a word since that day. Her therapists just keeps telling us to give her time and space, that she will talk in her own time. While Lola didn't witness everything that happened that day, she witnessed more than any four-year-old should!

"There is my favorite niece," I say when Lola walks into the kitchen dragging her Mystery Machine blanket and holding her Scooby Doo stuffed animal.

Reed shifts in his seat. Always unsure of himself now when it comes to Lola. "Have you decided what you want to do for your birthday this year, Princess?"

Lola shakes her head no.

I put a finger to my chin. "We have two weeks to figure it out, so we need to brainstorm. Let's fill the pool with Jello and everyone dress as fruit. We can call it the 'Mello Jello Bash.'"

Lola doesn't even smile as she shakes her head.

I shake my head too. "You are right, that sounds like a party for a nursing home. Ok. Want to do a tea party? No, let's do a circus theme. Sock hop! Mermaid party?"

Lola drops her head and tears start running down her cheeks before she runs out of the kitchen.

I turn to Reed. "Were my ideas that bad?"

Reed shakes his head. "No. Lola and Sandy would play mermaids anytime they were in a pool."

I run a hand down my face. "I am so sorry. I should go apologize to her."

Reed puts a hand on my arm. "You couldn't have known. Don't apologize and don't beat yourself up over it."

I nod. "Yeah, you are right, I guess. Ok. Well, I have to head to work. Think about where you want to go for dinner tonight."

I walk out to my truck, open the back door, lift the back seat and go to grab for the hidden bottle that I have replaced twice now. Maybe just a little added to my coffee this morning will be enough to ease the sting of making my niece cry. I am so stupid. I need to make a mental note to ask Reed tonight what Lola and Sandy played so I know not to make that mistake again. As I reach for the bottle, the blanket that I carelessly threw back there scratches my arm.

Should I have taken that second cab last night? Yes. I know the risks I put people in. After Quinn left, the emotions of all that had happened hit me again without a beautiful woman to distract me, so I apologized to the guy driving the second cab and handed him two twenties as an extra apology for wasting his time. Yet another reminder that everything that happened is my fault. If I would have never thought with my dick, Reed never would have met Gina in the first place, but that gave him Lola, so I won't wish that away. If I hadn't done it again, though, he would have first met Sandy as his nanny and would have never allowed himself to look at her as a love interest. But no, I had to drag him to the beach that day, lying about something happening in my life to guilt him into going. Just like I guilted him into going on that damn double date all those years ago. I grab the bottle and pour a heavy-handed shot into my coffee.

******

"Callie put her official resignation in. She is staying to train the new nurse and then heading to New Mexico," our chatty receptionist, Barbara, says as I walk into the teachers' lounge to top off my coffee.

"She has been saying for a while that it was coming. I hope she loves her new school. I am sad to see her go," I say.

Barbara slides in close to me. "I hope she changes her mind between now and then. I have met that fiancé of hers twice now and I don't like him. Not one bit. His eyes roam when he has the most beautiful woman on earth hanging onto his arm. Shady, shady man," she tsks.

I glance down at the older, feeble woman beside me. "Barbara, he must have some redeeming qualities if Callie chose him. She has a good head on her shoulders. We should trust her decision. Don't you think?"

Barbara shakes her head, causing a few white whisps to fall from her loose chignon. "I look at all of you like my own littles. Mama hearts don't stop wanting to protect their littles, even when they are grown and this mama heart has the luck of having many grown littles." She leans her head against my arm and gives it a pat. "And you, dear, are at the top of my list of my grown littles that I worry about. You know I am here if you ever need me."

I lean my head down and rest a cheek on Barbara's head. "I know you are. I am still doing okay."

"I don't believe you, but I can't force you into doing anything you aren't ready for. Just know that when that day comes, I am here."

I give her a squeeze on her arm before heading to the door. "Let's change little lives today, guys."

******

Even after throwing out a million ideas, Lola opted to just have her birthday party at the house with only Reed, Avery, James, Chris, and me in attendance. Avery and James were nice enough to bring the devil cat, Lucy Fur, and her side kick Cleocatra over for Lola to love on. If I weren't already a dog person, these cats would have forced me into being one. If they aren't fighting all over the place and creating a mess in their wake, they are purposefully knocking things off of counters and tables. I can confidently say it is purposefully because they will stare right at you as they do it. Like they are waiting for you to try to stop them, even though it would be futile. Or maybe they just hate me.

That could be it too. But they are the only things in the world that bring a smile back to Lola's face now.

Reed and I took her to the local shelter to see if she wanted to bring a pet home. Her therapist mentioned that having a pet to find comfort with could help speed her recovery along and we are desperate to just gain an inch, but she didn't connect to any of the cats or dogs. I even took her to see a goat. Do I want a goat? No. But if that would help her, by God, I would be the best goat uncle this world has ever seen.

"Hey, love birds, you brought the entertainment," I say, pointing to the cats in their carrier.

Avery sets the carrier down and swings the door to it open. "We brought Lola's favorite friends over to celebrate her birthday." Avery reaches in her oversized purse and pulls out a handful of headbands with cat ears on them. "Don't worry, Brad. I brought enough for everyone."

Lola's eyes light up when Avery walks over and places cat ears and a kiss to the top of her head. I watch Lola's hands come up to Avery's face and give Avery's cheeks a soft rub. I am instantly jealous. The most I have received was a pat on the hand and Reed, a hug to the leg but she would turn her head away from him when she did. She knows that we hold the blame for what happened.

Avery walks back to the rest of us, placing the headbands on our heads while James slowly makes his way to Lola. "Happy birthday, Princess," he says as he leans down to give her a soft hug, which she accepts. When James stands, I don't miss the way Lola's eyes trail to his stomach and widen before she walks over to the table.

"Where is Chris?" Avery asks.

"Running a little behind. Apparently, there was a mix up at the bakery and Lola's cake was sent to the wrong customer. I guess we both ordered the same cake with only the name being different. They are fixing it and then she will be heading here," Reed says.

Avery nods. "Sweet! I need to ask her a question when she gets here."

"I don't want to put Chris out. I will find a temporary rental. Chris has a one bedroom that is smaller than ours," James says.

Reed looks between Avery and James. "What's going on?"

James sighs. "Jack was supposed to move down in two months, but the job opened sooner than expected. I found an apartment a few blocks away, had everything lined up and I guess when the current tenant was doing their move out clean, they used the wrong cleaner in the oven causing a minor fire. So, the move in date is pushed back by a few weeks, obviously. Anyway, I want to have a place lined up before I say anything because I don't want to add any more stress to Jack's life right now."

Reed glances at me.

I point to the bedroom next to mine. "We have a spare room still."

James shakes his head. "You guys have enough on your plate. I don't want you to feel obligated to say yes just because it's for my kid."

I shake my head. "It is no problem at all. Besides, I think you would like for your kid to be close without being in your home. I swear I can hear you and Avery from here some nights."

James blushes and Avery howls out a laugh. "Don't be jelly, Brad," she says.

My mind drifts back to Quinn with her legs wrapped around my waist, looking down at me with lust filled eyes.

"I appreciate it. Between school, work, and well, me, Jack has been a little overwhelmed. You guys are doing me a solid. Let me know how much to rent the room from you and it's a deal," James says, reaching for his wallet.

"Free ninety-nine, man. We are family," I say.

James nods. "Thank you."

The front door opens and in walks Chris looking more disheveled than I have ever seen her.

"Are you okay?" I ask her as I rush over to grab the cake from her.

She pushes her hair back off of her face. "Of course. Why do you ask?"

"Your clothes are wrinkled and crooked," I say pointing towards her skirt.

Chris' cheeks blush.

Avery drops her hands to her knees, crouches down, and starts giggling uncontrollably. All eyes turn to her.

Avery points to Chris. "You and the baker?"

Chris's blushed cheeks go impossibly redder.

"I have to know, Chris. The dark-haired guy with the super bushy eyebrows or the lighter brunette with the gigantic hands. Judging by your clothes and your cheeks, I would say gigantic hand guy."

Chris shakes her head. "Neither."

Avery cocks her head to the side. "The only other person that works there is Candace, the…ohhhhhhh. I'm picking up what you are throwing down now. Why did I not know?"

We all look between Chris and Avery.

James is the one who finally has the balls to ask the question on all of our minds. "Know what?"

Chris's eyes dart between all of us. "Well, now that I have been practically shoved out," she says glaring at Avery, "Candace and I have been seeing each other on and off for the better half of a year."

Reed walks over to hug Chris. "Why didn't you tell me sooner?"

Chris glances at Reed. "Because you are still my boss."

Reed guffaws, "Like that changes anything?" He pulls her back in for a hug before releasing her.

I walk over next, throw my arm around her neck, and pull her in for a noogie. "So, when do we get to meet her on an official level?" I ask.

Chris straightens out her hair. "When you promise not to embarrass me and so far, you have proven my choice to keep it quiet was a good one."

James walks over next with a one-armed hug. "Glad you were finally ready to tell us all."

Chris looks at him with wide eyes. "I really wasn't, but how did you know?"

James taps his head. "Dad senses."

Chris rolls her eyes.

James chuckles. "And I saw your date in Chicago. She was very pretty but seemed stuck up."

"She was extremely stuck up." Chris laughs, looking around to make sure Lola is not within ear shot. "But she could do amazing things with her tongue."

I lean against the counter, propping my chin on my fist. "Please go into every detail."

Avery smacks me across the back of my head before walking over to Chris. Putting a set of cat ears on Chris, she loops their arms together and leads her out of the kitchen. "Let's let the boys simmer in their fantasies while you and I go play with our Princess. I brought the kitties."

"Chris's favorite thing to play with," I jest.

Chris flips me the bird over her shoulder as she and Avery saunter out of the room.

Reed claps his hands together. "Let's go start the grill. James, grab drinks. Brad, tape your mouth shut or something. I'll cook."

Chapter 5
Quinn

"Oh, come the fuck on. You have got to be kidding me," I say to the line of cars backed up in front of me on the highway clogging up the exit I need to take. I overslept. I had planned to leave Orlando by five this morning so I could have a quiet ride in and beat morning traffic, but I didn't wake up until five. The person at the desk when I went to check out was finger pecking the keyboard at a turtle's pace and the traffic was already getting bad before I even made it three exits down. This is the worst start to the first day of my new job. I knew I should have just finished out the last hour of the drive last night, but I wanted one last night of solitude before my entire world changed. Why did I ever listen to me? Horrible decision.

Once I finally get through my exit, I speed the entire rest of the way. Thankfully, I don't pass any cops on my way in, because running at over a hundred miles per hour would have been a hefty ticket. Possibly worse than that, but I am trying to look at everything as glass half full today. When I arrive at the school and park, I run inside while trying to balance everything I carried in, on, and under one arm.

When I get to the receptionist desk, I push my hair back from my forehead and reach out to shake her hand. "Hi, I'm Quinn, the new school nurse."

The white-haired lady looks from my face to the helmet under my arm, then the black jacket, black pants, and leather boots.

I drop my hand and glance down. "Sorry, I am running a little late today. If you could point me in the direction of a bathroom I could change in, I would greatly appreciate it."

Silently, the white-haired lady points behind her to an employee bathroom. I slide in and repeat my mantra to myself in the mirror while I shuck off my riding gear to put on my less intimidating shirt, maxi skirt, and cardigan outfit. "You can't rule the day, only your attitude. Your glass is half full and will never get full if you don't pour into it. Now get out there and pour, baby, pour."

I walk out of the bathroom with my riding gear in my bag and my helmet hanging from it. "Thank you for your assistance. Could I trouble you once more? Can you point me down which hallway to go to find Callie?"

The white-haired lady perks up at hearing Callie's name. "You know Callie?"

I nod. "Yes, we have been friends since Jr. High. She got me this job to replace her."

The white-haired lady comes out from behind her desk, and I find that she isn't much taller than my five-foot self. She puts out her hand to shake mine finally. "My name is Barbara; I'll walk you over to her office."

I shake her hand back and smile. "Thank you, Barbara. Lead the way."

I follow Barbara down a maze of hallways, catching glimpses inside classrooms here and there. This building is old, but you can see that they have updated the interior quite a bit since the few times I came over here for basketball games as a kid. Cal sucked at it but thought he was going to be the next Michael Jordan when he was in Jr. High. I would always ride with Callie to the games, and we would run the halls and sneak into classrooms. We thought we were total badasses until we got caught one time at this very school. They scared us into acting right when they threatened to expel us. Had Callie not been drawing dicks all over the chalkboards, I feel like we would have just had a slap on the wrist and no threats, but that wasn't the case.

"Her door is that one at the end there to the left. If you need anything else, you know where my desk is," Barbara says before heading back the way she just brought me.

I walk toward Callie's closed door and knock.

"Come on in." I hear Callie singsong from the other side.

I crack the door open and see that she has a grown man on the table, his back to me while she glances up from his head and smiles at me.

"Jackie-O. Come on in. I am almost finished with this big baby here," Callie says.

I drop my bag and helmet on a nearby chair and wave a hand in her direction. "No, it is fine. I will wait out here while you finish up."

The man on the table speaks up. "It's fine. Callie is almost done torturing me."

Callie looks down at the man. "Torturing? It was alcohol free antiseptic, B. Don't be a wimp!" She smacks his arm playfully before collecting the trash from the butterfly strips she used, and turning to walk them to the trash can.

The man on the table turns to defend his choice of words but stares at me with his mouth wide open, probably mirroring my expression.

Callie grabs his face and turns him back to face her so she can check her handiwork. "As long as you don't take any more harmonicas to the forehead this morning, you should be okay. What do you think, Jackie-O?"

I shake my head and make my way to stand in front of Brad to take a quick glance at the butterfly strips. "Looks solid."

Brad is still staring at me and not saying a word.

Callie pats his shoulder. "You okay there, B?"

Brad nods, eyes never leaving mine.

Callie shakes her head. "Oh my gosh. I am so rude. Brad, this is my friend Jacqueline, or Jackie-O as I like to call her. Though, she has adopted a new nickname, Quinn. She will be taking my spot when I leave."

Brad's eyes find mine. "Why Jackie-O?"

Callie giggles. "Because of her unique fashion choices growing up. She never followed the newest trends. Always just did her own thing clothing wise."

I look down at my boring ensemble and remember the crazy outfits I used to wear before college made me feel like I had to conform to fit in and make friends. I let out a soft laugh. "I really did. I should consider bringing back my Jackie-O flair."

"I bet you ten dollars that you won't," Brad says softly.

I smirk and my eyes meet his. "I bet you twenty I will just so I can take your money."

Brad holds a hand out and says, "I'll take that bet."

The second our hands meet, I feel the heat from that night flooding my body again.

"Alrighty then, B. You are good to go," Callie says. "Nurse Jackie-O and I have a lot to get to today."

Brad winks at me. "It was nice to meet you, Nurse Quinn? Nurse Jackie? Great TV show by the way. One of my favorites."

"It was. Nurse Quinn is fine. It was nice to meet you, too, Brad."

Callie reaches into a drawer and grabs a set of keys out of it before shooing us out the door. "Let's go get you all set up in the main office and then we will come back here to start going over where I keep health plans, individualized education program files, and all the rest of the logistical side of things."

Brad walks in front of us, sneaking a peek back our way with a small wave while Callie locks the door behind us and puts her "be back soon" sign on the door. She looks down at her watch and then back up to the sign and changes the hands on the clock to reflect thirty minutes from now.

******

By the time Callie and I are done for the day, my brain feels like mush. The parking lot is nearly empty as we walk towards her car and my bike. Her assigned spot is right next to the ramp accessible handicap spot. She left enough space for me to park in between her car and the sidewalk since there are no other teachers who drive in on bikes here.

"So, in the morning, I park here and just drink my coffee until all my wheelchaired students arrive. I stay out here and help get them out of their vehicles to make it a little easier on the parents. Many of them are barely making it to work on time as it is with school and work starting so close together, so if I can shave four minutes off their trip by being the one to load and unload, I do it," Callie tells me.

I look at her in awe. "You always have had the biggest heart. I never would have thought of something so simple being so impactful."

Callie looks down at her chest. "Why do you think I was blessed with such big boobs? Had to have some cushion to protect this big heart."

I look down at my own chest. "So that is why they grow big, huh? Glad to know there was a medical reason for my membership in the itty-bitty-titty committee," I laugh out.

"I never said it was a fair trade. I have to run, Trevor is already going to be upset that I am running late. I swear, if dinner isn't on the table by 5:45 P.M., he turns into a gremlin who ate after midnight," Callie says as she shuffles through her purse for her keys.

I shake my head. "Then he should start cooking now since today was a one-off kind of day for you."

Callie scoffs. "Trevor, cook? Ha! I don't think he could boil water if his life depended on it." She pulls out her keys. "Want me to bring you a coffee in the morning? Iced mocha still?"

I put my backpack on and get my helmet prepped. "That sounds perfect! I would absolutely love that. See you tomorrow morning, babe!"

I watch Callie pull out of her parking spot, pull down my helmet, and type in the address for where I am heading. I am so ready for a meal and a bed.

Chapter 6
Brad

I hear the rumble of a motorcycle outside. "Reed, Lola. Jack is here. Let's go greet him."

Reed walks out of his room. "James said he will be down in a few minutes. Guess he heard the bike from over there too. Rob and Dob are going to love our newest roommate."

I scoff. "You really need to talk to Rob. He will tell you all of his wild stories. Some of which include him and his wife riding a motorcycle out to Sturgis a few times."

Reed looks towards the side of the house that neighbors Rob's house. "I really should. She would be so mad at me for being right here and not going over there."

I pat him on the shoulder. "Avery has been keeping up with him. Don't beat yourself up. Now come on. Let's go greet Jack. Princess, you coming?"

Lola peeks around the corner of her doorway before slowly walking out and waddling into the living room. I jog over to the front door, swing it open, and we all watch in amazement as Jack dismounts his Harley. His? Wait.

I look towards Reed and whisper, "You see them too, right?"

Reed looks at me quizzically. "See what?"

I bounce my eyes back to Jack's chest before looking back at Reed. "Dude, James' son has boobs."

"Jack is a girl you idiot," Reed laughs out.

I feel the blood drain from my face. "What? No. Jack. Boy name."

Reed claps my back. "Jack. Short for Jacqueline."

My stomach falls to my feet. This can't be happening. James will kill me. No, he will torture me and take pleasure in it if he knew the obscene thoughts I have had of his daughter. I should prepare myself for life as a eunuch.

I watch in horror as "Jack" removes her helmet and I am staring at my Jellyfish. My dream woman. Walking up to my house…where she will sleep in the room right next to mine. I look up to the ceiling and curse this joke that the universe has decided to play on me. I am Eve and she is the forbidden fruit dangling in front of me at work and now at home too.

Lola pushes her way between me and Reed at this moment, and I can see her eyes go wide. Not from fear or anxiety but from being intrigued. I watch my Jellyfish's eyes go straight to Lola, naturally, and a huge smile takes over her face.

"Lola! I haven't seen you since you were a baby! Look at how tall you have gotten." Quinn's eyes raise to me and Reed, and she stops.

"Get over here, Jack. Where is my hug?" Reed asks, obviously not picking up on the elephant on the front porch.

Quinn opens her arms and walks over to Reed. "I am glad to see you doing well. Dad has kept me up to date with most things. But how are you, truly?"

Reed gives Quinn a tight squeeze. "Don't worry about me, kid. I am doing what I need to do to heal. My therapist is proud of the little bit of progress we have made so far. I have good days and bad days like all of us, but I know that one day we will heal from it all."

I don't miss how his eyes fall to Lola with that last sentence.

"Jack! How was your first day?" I hear James ask from the driveway.

Quinn spins around to jog over to him and give him a big hug. "Hey, Dad. It was good! Callie said your ass is grass when she sees you next for not reaching out to her."

James huffs out a laugh. "She would absolutely beat me in a fight right now. Plan a weekend brunch and tell me the day. My treat to both of you girls."

Avery runs across Rob's yard with her arms open wide. "Jackie! Oh my gosh, I am so glad to see you! Your father is driving me nuts. He is trying to say he is done with physical therapy, and he doesn't need it anymore. Do the puppy dog eye thing you do so he will stop being ridiculous."

I watch Quinn and Avery hug like they are best friends. I feel like the butt of the cruelest joke right now. Everyone knows each other and yet for weeks, I have been praying to every God and higher being known to man to let me see her again. All of them answered me at once, now that I can't have a future with her.

James points to where Reed, Lola, and I are still standing in the doorway. "I am sorry it took me so long to get over here. I had to fight Cleo to get my shoe. She really didn't want to give it up. Let's go in and get you settled. You know Reed. Did you meet Brad?"

I point to the bandages on my forehead. "Yeah, Quinnie here assisted in making sure I was patched up today at school."

Quinn glances over at me. "You are giving me more credit than I deserve. I just checked Callie's work."

I walk towards where Quinn, James, and Avery are standing. "Where are your things? I will start carrying everything in for you."

Quinn leans forward and opens one of her saddlebags, pulling out a toiletry bag and a small duffle bag. "This is it for now. My movers won't be here until tomorrow at the earliest. A flat slowed them down and they can't get a replacement tire until tomorrow morning. Avery, can I borrow something to sleep in? I didn't think to pack an extra sleep set."

Avery says, "Of course."

At the same time, I say, "You can borrow something of mine."

Quinn looks between me and Avery.

James breaks the silence. "Let's get you settled inside, and we can chat about it in there."

We all turn to walk inside. Lola hanging out by the door until all of us have come in.

Quinn circles back to Lola and holds her hand out. "Want to show me my room?"

Lola stares at her outstretched hand for a minute before grabbing it and silently leading her down the hallway.

Reed, James, Avery, and I all stop. Holding our breaths as we watch Lola lead Quinn away. I turn to the three of them. Avery's hand is covering her mouth as tears silently fall down her cheeks. James has the look of a proud dad mixed with what I can only describe as hope. Reed looks numb for a second before plastering a fake smile on his face.

"I am going to go order some Chinese food for dinner. I will just get a large spread of things," Reed says as he walks out of the living room.

James turns to follow him, but Avery stops him. "Give him a moment, Honey. He just watched his baby take her first step in a way. Just…give him a minute."

James nods and I open an arm towards the hallway. "Ladies first."

******

It is after midnight, and I just keep tossing and turning. I never got a chance to talk to Quinn alone and it is messing with my sleep now. After dinner, she went over to Avery and James' house to raid Avery's closet. Lola opted to go with them so that she could see the cats. Reed and I couldn't do anything but watch as Lola grabbed Quinn's hand again before they left the house. Quinn didn't even glance down at her. She just wrapped her fingers around

Lola's little hand like it was habit. Once they were out of sight, Reed dropped his head and then went to his room. I know this is tearing him apart and that he is trying to keep up the façade that he is strong and okay.

When Quinn and Lola came back, I intercepted Lola in the living room. I told them Reed was tired and had fallen asleep already before taking Lola to her room to start her bedtime routine. By the time Lola was asleep, Quinn was already in her room with the door shut so I was not about to invade her privacy or make her feel uncomfortable by knocking to talk to her tonight.

After flopping over four more times, I frustratedly stand up to head to the kitchen. I skipped any booze tonight and that is just what I need now to help me get to sleep.

I dig around the kitchen as quietly as I can as I pull out a small pot, a bottle of rum, milk, a cinnamon stick and the nutmeg. If I am going to have a drink to help me sleep, I might as well make it a tasty one. I am stirring the milk in the pot on the stovetop when I hear her shuffle in.

"Can't sleep?"

I glance behind me to see Quinn standing in the kitchen doorway in a pair of silky night shorts with a matching camisole. "Nope. I see you are having the same issue."

Quinn shrugs. "I always have trouble sleeping the first couple of nights in a new place. Every sound makes me think the place is haunted. Too many horror flicks I suppose."

I turn back to my stirring. "Take a seat, I will make you one of my favorite sleepy time drinks."

Quinn walks up to me and pats the counter. "Help me up, macho man?"

I smirk at her but do as she asks. I lower the heat on the stove before stepping directly in front of her. Her eyes roam over my bare chest. Scooting in a little closer, I grip her hips and slowly lift her up before depositing her on the counter. Her legs hanging on either side of mine. I lean in and feel her breathing go shallow as I reach above her for a second glass. Her hands find either side of my torso and cause goosebumps to cover my skin. I lean in, preparing to plant a kiss on her exposed neck that her messy bun blessed me with when she shifts back and clears her throat. I look at her face and then follow her line of sight.

"Princess. What are you doing up?" I ask even though I know she won't answer me.

Lola glances down and then waddles over to the counter to stand beside Quinn's dangling feet.

"You want some warm milk too?" I ask her.

She pats the counter in answer. I pick her up and sit her down next to Quinn.

"I like your Scooby," Quinn says, pointing to Lola's stuffed Scooby that she is gripping to her chest.

Lola looks down, admiring him, and then nods.

"Princess, do you want cinnamon in your milk tonight?" I ask her while I pour warm milk into two adult mugs and Lola's mini version of a coffee mug that I typically use for her chocolate milk that she likes to have with breakfast.

Lola looks at me for a second and then gives the slightest tip of one corner of her lip and a single nod of her head.

My chest swells and hurts all at the same time. I decide to skip the rum now that Lola is in here. I can't let her see that I am drinking. I know logically that it is okay to drink in moderation and teach kids that it is not shameful, but I never want her to see me drinking unless it is in a social setting.

Quinn holds up her mug and Lola follows her lead. "Brad, do you want to do the honors?"

I look at her confused.

Quinn waves her hand for me to bring my mug up to meet hers and Lola's. "To those who hurt, to those who heal, and to those of us who need help to feel…or sleep." Quinn taps our mugs, adding a wink when she clinks Lola's, and brings hers to her mouth.

Lola looks at Quinn, letting a half smile escape her control before bringing her child sized mug to her mouth.

I stare at the most important girl in my life admiring the woman who has been haunting my dreams. I lift my mug to my mouth and let my brain wander for just a few seconds about how this could be something I would enjoy: Having midnight milk dates with a wife and child of my own someday. This is the first time in months that I have allowed myself to think of any happy prospects for my future and it only takes a couple seconds before the guilt of it hits me.

"Let's get you back to bed, Princess. We all have school tomorrow," I say as I pick Lola up from the counter and place her on the ground.

Lola looks to Quinn and points to her like she is asking, "You have school too?"

Quinn nods. "I am the school nurse at the school where your uncle works."

I turn to face Quinn. "Lola is a kindergartener of ours." Crouching down in front of Lola, I tell her, "And if you need something and I can't help you, you can go to Nurse Quinn here and she will find me."

Lola looks between me and Quinn before she nods once and turns to go to her room.

I point down the hallway. "Let me go put her to bed. Are you going to be up for a bit?"

Quinn shakes her head. "No, I think your warm milk did the trick. Goodnight, Pookie."

I watch Quinn walking down the hallway. "Goodnight, Jellyfish."

I wait until I hear her bedroom door shut before making my way down the hallway towards Lola's room and tucking her back into bed. "Goodnight, Princess," I say to Lola before kissing her forehead.

Lola kisses her Scooby doll and then puts his nose to my cheek. I can't hide my smile as I get up and head out of her room. When I get to my bedroom door, I stand there for a second, staring at Quinn's bedroom door before finally entering my room and getting back in bed. At least when I do get to sleep tonight, I have a nice visual now to dream about.

Chapter7
Quinn

My alarm goes off at five and I roll out of bed. Grabbing my toiletry bag and my outfit for the day, I head to the bathroom. I walk in the first half of the bathroom that has two sinks, set my bag down, and grab the door handle for the door that leads into the other half of the bathroom that houses the toilet and shower. As soon as my hand grips the handle, the door flies open causing me to fall forward and land headfirst into a hard chest.

"Jelly, if you wanted to join me, all you had to do was ask," Brad says, helping to steady me.

I push the hair that fell out of my bun in my sleep out of my face and run my hand down my clothing like it will make me look any better at this ridiculous hour. "What are you doing in here? Don't you have a bathroom?"

Brad points to where Reed's bedroom is. "I gave Reed the bigger room with the en-suite when he and Lola moved in. She likes the jacuzzi tub. So, that leaves this bathroom for you and me to share, Jelly."

I look around the bathroom and blush. "I have never shared a living space with any guy but my dad."

"For fuck's sake Quinnie! Please never mention your father to me when I am nearly naked in a towel and you are dressed in a silk night set. Never. Again. Please."

I take a second to look Brad over now and it registers that he truly is just in a towel…a very small towel. One I would typically use as a hair towel and not one for my body. His thick and muscular thighs peek out from where the towel ends do not meet.

"If you keep staring at me like that, I will have to get back in the shower to handle some business. Cold if I am alone, hot if you are joining me," he says with a wink.

I smack his chest. "It is too early for you. I haven't even had coffee yet." I point to the shower. "May I?"

Brad nods. "Yeah, jump on in. I have to go get towels out of the dryer. I forgot to fold them last night and this was the last towel in here. I promise I will keep up with the towel laundry in the future. I will have them waiting on you before you get done."

I glance down at his little towel. "One that is bigger than that, right?"

Brad huffs. "God, I hope you are only referring to the towel right now."

A laugh escapes me. "Go. Let me shower so I can thaw myself. I have to have hot water scorch my outsides to bring my insides back to a normal temperature. Without that, I am the epitome of an ice queen."

"Yes ma'am," Brad says as he shuffles out of the bathroom.

I turn the water on and wait only a minute before stepping in. The water pressure in this shower is every woman's dream. Actually, this whole shower is. It has a good seal on the glass doors, so the heat is staying in while letting out the exact right amount of steam from the gap at the top. There is a seat in the corner so you can hike up a leg to shave out of the water while your other leg stays in the stream. It is when I am bent over shaving my leg that I hear a light tapping on the door.

"Yeah?" I call out.

Brad walks in carrying towels that he immediately drops.

I glance back to find Brad staring at my ass that is in the air. "Yeah was a question, not an invitation," I state.

"I… I… No. I asked if you wanted me to bring them in and you said 'Yeah.' Otherwise, I would not have just walked in here."

I continue shaving my leg. "Oh. Unfortunate time for some miscommunication. I didn't hear you. I'm sorry."

Brad's eyes are still glued to my ass. "Yeah, absolutely horrible. I'm… I'm just… are you going to accept my proposal anytime soon or are you still debating?"

I stand up and drop my leg, turning to the glass door and cracking it open. I don't need to, I know that he can see my bare, wet chest through the glass with how his eyes go wide. "I am still debating. I might be more tempted to say yes if a cup of coffee magically appeared next to my makeup bag. A little creamer or milk with a couple sugars if you don't have a flavored creamer."

"I would go find a cow and personally milk it if it would sway you towards a yes. Your coffee will be ready soon," he rasps out.

I reach a hand out of the shower, grab a fist full of Brad's sweatpants, and pull him towards me. With my other hand I reach up, grab the back of his neck, and pull his cheek down for me to kiss. "Mmmmmm, I could get used to this kind of treatment." I playfully push him away, shut the door, and keep my eyes locked on his as I step backwards under the spray again.

He reaches out to touch the glass, running his hand across it from where my chest is and down toward my stomach. "You are going to get me in so, so much trouble, Quinnie."

"Only if you get caught, Pookie. So don't get caught." I turn around so my back is to him and let the water warm me up again.

******

When I step out of the shower, I find a coffee sitting next to my makeup bag with a muffin on a plate. I shake my head and whisper to myself, "He is such a golden retriever." I finish getting ready, sporting the biggest grin I have worn since the night I met him.

After applying my make-up, blow drying my hair, and giving myself my "full cup" pep talk, I open the door and am startled by the little girl standing right outside of it. She is dressed in an adorable, green dress that nearly matches her eyes with her brown hair pulled up into a sloppy ponytail.

I point to her hair. "Want some help?"

She nods.

I wave her in. "Hmmmm, I think we need braids. This dress was made for some French braids. What do you think?"

Lola gives me a small smile and a nod.

I open my arms to her and say, "Alright then, let's get you on the counter so I can do this."

She walks over to me, hesitantly opens her arms, and lets me lift her to the counter before she spins around to watch me in the mirror. I see her glancing over at my muffin, so I slide it in front of her before I start. She lets a small smile slip again. Acting like I didn't see it, and I start talking.

"When I was your age, it was just me and my dad. I didn't have a mom around. While my dad is one of the best dads that has ever existed in this world, he was the worst at doing my hair. Did you know that he would suck my hair up into the vacuum cleaner hose?" I pause to see Lola's reaction before continuing, "he would. He would put my hairbow on the end of the hose where it sucks everything up, turn it on, suck my hair in, and then slide my hair bow down."

Lola softly giggles.

"Luckily, I had really sweet teachers who took pity on me and would braid my hair before school started. Some days, they would even let me practice braiding their hair so that I could learn how to do it for myself. It took me nearly a whole school year to learn how to do a single French braid, but once I learned how, that is the only way I would wear my hair for years." I finish one braid and move to the other side of her head to start the other one. "Then, in middle school, I met Callie, your school nurse whose position I am taking over. She is my best friend, and she has been since our first year of middle school. She taught me different ways to do my hair, how to blow dry to keep volume, how to curl, how to straighten my parts that like to go wavy on really humid days. I burned my hands and forehead too many times to count but eventually, I was a pro at it." I am braiding that last inch of her hair now. "And someday, you will know how to do all of that too."

Lola turns her head side to side, admiring her braids in the mirror before turning around to me. She brings both of her hands to my cheeks and rubs them.

"You are welcome, Little One. Now, let's go find the guys."

I help her off the counter and we walk to the kitchen, hand in hand. Brad and Reed are sitting at the kitchen table, Reed reading the newspaper and Brad scrolling some app on his phone.

"Good morning, guys," I say, leading Lola to the table.

Reed looks up from his paper. "Good morning, Jack. Good morning, Princess. Your hair looks lovely! Thank you, Jack."

I notice the slight flinch that Lola made when Reed called her Princess. "It was my pleasure, we needed a morning girl chat and that gave us time to have it." I wink at Lola, and she tries to wink back at me but just blinks one eye before the other.

Brad is watching Lola's wink blink with such intensity. He looks over at me before looking back at Lola. Stunned silent is the only way I could describe his facial expression. He stands abruptly. "I need to head to work."

Reed glances to the clock on the stove. "Dude, you have like thirty minutes before you have to leave."

Brad looks anxious. "Yeah, normally, but I have some stuff I was supposed to do yesterday and put off." Brad turns to me. "Text your dad, pick where we are all eating for dinner tonight. Reed's treat."

Reed whips his head towards Brad. "Oh, is it?"

Brad gives a cocky nod of his head. "Yep. It is Friday, Quinnie's welcome to our home and congrats on your new job dinner. You are the rich one, so it falls on you."

Reed laughs out, "Fine. Jack, pick where you want to go for dinner and tell your dad or Avery. One of us will add you to the family group chat today so that way you will have the pleasure of being annoyed by Brad and Avery having nonsensical arguments, but you will also be notified of dinner plans for most nights. We rarely have a night go by that we all don't get together for dinner since we are all living so close. Chris is in the group chat too. Did you ever meet her?"

I nod. "Yeah, I met her when Dad was in the hospital."

Reed and Brad both go a shade paler, and Lola drops her head.

I turn to Lola. "Little One."

Lola looks up at me.

"I don't know what is good to eat here anymore. Want to help me pick a place?"

Her face brightens and she gives the slightest tip of her lips.

"Great. Tell me after school where you think we should go." I turn to head to my room to grab my helmet, but Brad stops me.

"We are expecting a storm today. Want to ride with me?"

I look down at my watch. "Ummm, yeah, I suppose so. Thank you. I didn't even check the weather for today. Mind if I change into my skirt really quick? I never ride in anything but jeans or leathers. I promise I will be quick."

Brad nods. "Go do what you have to do. I'll meet you out here in a few minutes." He smacks my ass as I walk by and all I want to do at this point is drag him into my room. This tension has been building for far too long.

Chapter 8
Brad

After enjoying the view of Quinn's ass swaying down the hallway, I make my way to my room. I head straight to the drawer that hides my Rumple Minze. Is it my preferred numbing agent? No. But on workdays, it is my go to for a quick shot because of its minty smell. I stare at the bottle, silently berating myself for feeling like I need it and knowing that Sandy would kick my ass if she knew how I was coping with everything. I don't talk to Reed about it because he has enough on his plate. I can't turn to James and Avery because they have his healing and medical appointments to deal with on top of Avery losing her best friend. So, I have alcohol. It numbs the unbearable feelings enough to make them manageable while simultaneously giving me a dopamine hit that brings out my seemingly lost easy-going side.

I hear Quinn's bedroom door open and shut so I take a quick swig to numb the emotions brought on from watching Lola have a sliver of her old self back before watching the wall drop again. Leaving my room, I find Quinn and Lola in the hallway, so I stay in the shadows to hear what Quinn is saying to her to bring that lightness out again.

"Remember, if you need me, I will be in the nurse's office with Nurse Callie all day. You will have a great day; you will learn three cool things today and…" Quinn puts a finger to her chin in contemplation before continuing, "you will make one new friend today. Not just any friend. They will be your life-long best friend. Now, repeat it in your head. Manifest it, Little One. We have to create our own futures, and it starts here," Quinn points to Lola's heart, "and here." Quinn points to Lola's head.

Lola reaches out, grabs Quinn's hand and rubs it against her cheek. Quinn crouches down and kisses the back of Lola's hand. "Let's go have a great day."

I turn around and head back to my drawer. I need one more swig.

******

It is my week as a monitor in the cafeteria. Most teachers loathe their monitoring week, but I love mine. I love seeing the kid's eyes light up when they open their lunchboxes from home and find that their favorite treat is in there. Or when they have plain chips instead of BBQ, but their friend wants to trade them because they want plain chips instead of the BBQ chips they got that day. The kids walking from the lunch line with their little trays and getting excited when they see that their friends have saved a spot for them. Hearing their joy when they talk about the new show they watched, book they read, or what their weekend plans are. It is a reminder to step back and look at the world through little eyes.

My eyes flit across the cafeteria and find my Jellyfish sitting next to one of our girls who needs a little assistance with eating. Like she can sense me watching her, she lifts her head up and gives me a smile. It is the most beautiful sight in the world. I begin to make my way over to where she is, but I am stopped dead in my tracks when I hear the vilest sentence come from a child's mouth to my right.

"...that is why your mom went crazy and shot everyone."

Quinn must notice my face drop. She says something to Callie, who takes over assisting the little girl and Quinn quickly walks over to me.

"Brad, what is wrong? Are you okay?" She asks, grabbing my arm and pulling me towards the back of the cafeteria.

I shake my head and point towards where that little boy spoke. "I need to get Lola."

Quinn looks over my shoulder to find Lola who is sitting alone, silently crying. "I will get her. What happened?"

"A little boy…I didn't hear the first half of the sentence. Only the part where he mentioned Gina shooting people."

Quinn drops my arm and sprints towards Lola but before she gets to her, a little girl slides in beside Lola and throws an arm around her shoulder. Quinn stops abruptly and slowly walks to the opposite side of the table behind Lola. Close enough to listen in but far enough away to give Lola some space. Quinn's face goes from clenched jaw to a soft smile, and I take in a steadying breath.

I watch the little boy that made the comment. Once he is done eating and heading toward the door to go outside to the playground, I stop him and escort him to the principal's office. He can have fun explaining to the principal why he said what he said. I will ask Quinn what happened with the other little girl when we leave work later.

******

On the way home, Quinn animatedly tells me how the little girl that sat down with Lola, Dawn, comforted Lola and told her not to listen to the little boy. Dawn went on about how that boy is just a meany head who is mean to people because he is sad about something and wants everyone else to be sad, too. That Lola should not pay him her tears because they are expensive and she should save her tears for people who are worth the price. That is what her daddy told her and her daddy never lies so it has to be the truth. Then she went on to tell Lola that it was ok with her if Lola didn't want to talk because her daddy says she talks enough for everyone. Watching Quinn get so excited over Lola making a friend rubs off on me, making me excited to go home and see our little Princess.

When we walk in, we find Reed and Lola sitting on the couch with Avery. Lola's eyes are red and puffy. Reed turns to face me and Quinn.

"What happened to her today?" He barks out.

I instinctively step in front of Quinn. "Calm down. Lola had a run in with a shit of a kid. He was handled by the principal. He said something truly awful." I look at Lola and wait for her to meet my stare. "And what he said, was completely out of line."

Quinn steps in front of me. "Remember what Dawn said about sad people?"

Lola nods at her.

Quinn crouches. "Is he worth the expensive tears?"

Lola shakes her head and pulls her shoulders back.

Quinn nods. "That is right, Little One. Now, where did you decide on for dinner?"

Lola runs to the drawer I keep take out menus in and shuffles through them before pulling one out for a place that most kids would never choose.

Quinn looks down at the menu and lets out a soft giggle. "This is your pick? This is where you want to go?"

Lola pushes the orange and white menu into Quinn's hand.

"Well then, looks like it's a wings kind of night and a nice view for the guys."

Reed glances over Quinn's shoulder at the menu. "Lola, when have you ever had food from there?"

Lola looks my way, followed by all the other eyes in the room.

I shrug and point to Lola. "All the well-endowed ladies love Lola. They spend more time at the table when she is with me. Besides, Lola truly does like their wings."

Reed shakes his head, Avery lets out a laugh, Lola looks around in confusion, and Quinn smirks.

Avery quells her laughing long enough to say, "I'll let James know where to meet us. I am sure he will enjoy the chesticles after being stuck around all the testicles at his physical therapy appointment."

******

By the time we make it home from dinner, Lola is barely awake. Reed takes her to his room to let her bathe, leaving me and Quinn in the living room.

"Well, that was a fun dinner," Quinn says, pulling her hair down from the ponytail she had it in.

"I tried telling you guys that the women there love Lola. I swear, every time I take her, she gets a minimum of two desserts on the house. There was one day, they brought one of every appetizer for her to try until she found one she liked."

She laughs and plops down on the couch. "I am sure you enjoyed the views when they did that."

I shake my head. "Maybe before but nothing beats the view I had tonight."

Quinn leans back. "The blonde or the red head?"

I shake my head again. "The raven haired one."

Quinn cocks her head to the side. "I don't recall seeing anyone that wasn't blonde, ginger, or mousy brunette in there."

I kneel down in front of where Quinn is sitting. "How could I look at any other woman in the room when you were sitting in front of me, Jelly? I couldn't take my eyes off of you." I lean in and kiss above her knee before standing.

I don't make it a step before Quinn reaches out and grips my Chinos. I look down at her hand and slowly follow up the length of her arm, to her neck to see that her pulse is picking up, then to her bottom lip she is chewing on, up to her lust filled eyes. I let her pull me back to her, pull me down on the couch beside her, where she takes control, and straddles me.

"I think we should pick up where we left off on Valentine's Day. You know, the part of what would have happened if we had shared a cab that night," she says, leaning forward to kiss my neck.

"I think you are right. We really should," I say, grabbing her ass in my hands. "We have two options, we wait for Lola to go to bed and then stay as quiet as possible, or we go for a walk down to this lifeguard stand that I know is out of commission."

Quinn leans back. "Mmmm voyeurism. Kinky. Let's go."

I shoot Reed a text letting him know that we are going for a walk, grab Quinn's hand, and rush out the door.

Chapter 9
Quinn

The excitement rushing through me as we walk up the ramp to the abandoned lifeguard stand is off the charts. Brad opens the door and leads me in before placing a cinderblock against the door to hold it shut.

"Bring all your dates up here, Pookie?" I ask, glancing around at the table and chair in the corner that holds a couple of used candles on it.

"Only the ones I ask to marry me," he says nonchalantly.

"You brought Patsy here?" I ask, turning my back to the desk.

He slowly stalks toward me. "No, Jelly. You, just you. You are the only woman I have ever brought here. Usually, I come here alone," he says before stopping in front of me.

I reach out, grab his shirt, and begin to lift it over his head until he takes over and yanks it off. "I see."

He watches as my fingers lower to the buttons on his pants. "Fuck. I don't have protection. It's at the house."

I lift a finger to his lips to shush him. Reaching into the pocket of my jeans, I pull out a condom, and wave it between us.

"Do you just carry one around everywhere?" He asks me.

I finish unbuttoning his pants and push them down to the ground, his boxers following shortly after. "I knew before my shower ended this morning that I was going to fuck you at some point today, so I stayed prepared." I stare at Brad's rock-hard dick for a second in appreciation. "Now then, are we going to talk? Or are we going to fuck?"

Brad bends down, his mouth finding mine in a desperate hunger. His fingers work quickly to unbuckle my jeans, pulling them down along with my panties. He pulls back long enough to lift my shirt over my head before picking me up and placing me on the desk. I hand him the condom watching as he rips the package open and rolls it on himself. I watch the way his muscles in his abs, arms and legs move as he does so. He steps forward, notching his head against my pussy.

"I'll go easy on you, Jelly," he says as he leans over and kisses me tenderly on my neck.

I push him against the chair, forcing him to fall onto the seat. "If I wanted easy, we would have stayed at the house," I say, mounting him. As I drop myself down on him fully, I hear his appreciative whispers while my head falls back from the pure stinging pleasure of taking him so fast. His mouth finds my tits, and I begin to move.

"Use your teeth," I breathe out.

When he does, I can't contain the moan that leaves my lips. I start riding him harder, our pants getting shorter. His thumb finds my clit, the pressure sends me over the edge and into my first orgasm.

"God, yes. Cum for me, Quinnie. You are so fucking beautiful when you cum."

When I have come down, I slow my rhythm on top of him, but he isn't ready to slow down yet. He loops his hands under my knees. "Hold on tight, Quinnie."

I do as he says, and he stands, pushing my back up against a wall.

"Oh, fuck yes," I grit out.

He starts thrusting up into me and at this angle he is so deep inside me. I am not used to not being the one in control, but I am loving this change up. I move my hands from around his neck to the back of his head, gripping into his hair. "Yes. Just like that. Fuck me hard. Use me, Brad. Take it all out on me, just like this."

Brad leans his head against my chest and starts pounding me impossibly harder. I can barely catch my breath when the next orgasm takes over me. As I clench around his cock, Brad lets out an animalistic grunt before falling forward, pinning me tightly between him and the wall until he has a chance to catch his own breath.

He pulls back from me and looks down into my eyes. "Now will you marry me?"

I smack his chest and laugh. "Put me down."

He pulls me off of his cock and sets me down on the desk again. I watch him remove the condom, tie it up, and toss it into the trash can on the other side of the desk. I lean back on my elbows, legs dangling off the side of the desk, in my full naked glory and watch Brad dress.

"Are you just going to watch me or are you going to get dressed too?"

I sit up straight. "I was just enjoying the view, but if you prefer I dress, I suppose I can."

Brad growls. "Oh, I don't want you to ever be dressed around me again but unfortunately, that is not an option at the moment. We should get back soon if we want the 'we went on a walk' excuse to be believable."

I stand and walk to my clothing, bending seductively to pick them up, ass on display in front of Brad before stepping into my pants. "Whatever you say, Pooks."

******

My belongings finally arrive on Saturday afternoon and Brad offered to take me to the storage unit holding them all so I could grab a few things I would need over the next couple of weeks. That turned into a quickie on my couch in the storage unit. Brad now carries a stash of condoms in his truck, and two in his wallet at all times.

"Reed and Lola will be going out of town over spring break. We will have a whole week to ourselves."

I pick my head up from the box I am digging through. "I think I get my place the weekend before or after. I don't remember. I will have to check the messages. Regardless, I will trade you a week of sex if you help me move my things when the time comes. Deal?"

Brad walks over to where I am sitting, crouches down, kisses my head and says, "Deal."

I sniff the air. "Do you smell… is that Rumple Minze? Brad, have you been drinking?"

Brad shakes his head. "Must be my mouthwash."

I shrug. "Weird. So, Callie wants to get together tonight for a going away meet up. Want to join?"

Brad moves the box I just closed against the wall. "Yeah, what's the plan?"

I open the next box. "Some country bar. It's on the mainland. She sent me the address earlier."

Brad stands. "Yeah, I know which one it is. I am going to grab my bottled water out of the truck, want yours?"

I wipe my brow. "Yeah, that sounds good."

When Brad comes back, I swear I catch a hint of Rumple on his breath, but I know he is drinking water. I shrug it off as my nose playing tricks on me.

"So, tonight. Do you want to take an Uber so we don't have to worry about driving?" I ask.

He shoots me that panty dropping grin. "I'll stay sober. You party it up with your bestie and I will get you home safely."

I get up and make my way over to where he is sitting, drop down to straddle him and kiss him deeply. "Get me home safe tonight and I will make sure you are very, very, happily rewarded," I say as I slide off of him, leaving my hand to trail over his hardening cock behind me.

******

Pulling up in front of the bar, I let out a soft laugh.

"Penny for your thoughts?" Brad asks.

I shake my head. "When Callie and I were younger, she would always tell me how excited she was to someday be old enough to go to an old country saloon and be swept around the dance floor by some cowboy."

"Did she ever get that moment?"

I lift an eyebrow. "You have met Trevor. They have been together since high school. Do you think she ever got to live that moment?"

Brad cringes. "Got it: pipe dream."

I grunt. "I truly dislike him, you know. No, I hate him. He may be the only person on that list, but he definitely made it to that one."

"Same. I have only met him once and wasn't a fan. Let's head in and try to have some fun. I may not be a cowboy, but I can spin her around the floor a couple of times."

I turn to Brad. "Ummm, before we go in. I don't think we should be us tonight. I just started this job and don't want people thinking I am already working my way through the teachers."

Brad nods. "Okay, you are ashamed of me." He pats his heart and whispers, "It's okay, big guy. We can handle the rejection." He gazes over at me with a smile and then drops it into a fake frown. "Tonight, I am just the lonely music teacher pining over the hottest nurse who doesn't want to play naughty nurse with him."

I smack his arm. "You will get the naughty nurse if you act right tonight."

"Let's make this quick then because I can't promise much knowing that when we get home, I get to have you again."

I shake my head, open my door and jump down from his truck. I glance behind me as I make it to the door to see him still sitting in the driver's seat. He waves me forward, points down to his crotch, and then waves for me to walk in again.

I find Callie standing at the bar with Josh, their old neighbor. I had no idea that Josh and Callie were close enough that she would invite him to her going-away party. I walk up from behind and throw my arms around her. "Quick, Josh, go grab the balloons from her table. Let me tie her up to this barstool so she can't leave me."

Callie laughs out, "I promise I will come back to visit. My brother still lives here after all."

"Speaking of, will he be gracing us with his presence tonight?" I ask.

Callie nods toward a hallway. "Yeah, once he is done in the pisser."

"Can you please talk like a lady in public?" Trevor chastises.

I turn in his direction. "Pisser was the lady-like way to say it. Shitter is my preferred term. Josh, what is yours?" I ask over my shoulder, eyes still locked on Trevor's.

"I prefer the Australian term 'dunny.' It is just fun to say," Josh states.

"The Australians know how to name a bathroom: Thunderbox. I mean, nothing beats that," Brad says, coming to stand behind me.

Josh nods in agreement and Callie snorts. Trevor just looks annoyed and walks to the table decorated with balloons and streamers. Cal walks out of the hallway and waves in our direction. As he steps closer, I throw my arms out wide for a hug.

"Flapjack! Look at you!" Cal exclaims as he pulls me in tightly. "Who would have thought that in the few years you were gone, you would grow up and finally look like a woman."

I pat Cal's stomach after he pulls away. "And who would have thought that you would finally gain some muscles."

Cal flexes his arms. "I had to do something to kill off the boredom after you left me and Callie became a housewife when she wasn't working."

Callie groans. "Homebody, Cal. I am just a homebody. Just as I have always been. We just don't share the same home anymore, so now it annoys you."

Cal shrugs. "Whatever you say. Let's get some shots going. Brad, you in?"

Brad shakes his head. "Nah, I am Quinnie's chauffer tonight. Just water for me."

Brad and I follow Callie over to the table while Josh stays back with Cal to carry shots.

It only takes a few rounds for all of us, but Brad, before we are a loud and rowdy bunch. The bar is packed and everyone is having fun. Even Trevor has actually laughed a few times.

"Callie, can I have this dance?" Brad asks.

Callie nervously looks at Trevor before looking back at Brad and sheepishly agreeing. Before Brad and Callie even make it to the dance floor, Trevor starts grumbling about how embarrassing it is to have a fiancé that dances with other men. To avoid commenting on how his small dick energy is stifling, I stand and head to the bar. I will just hang out there until Brad and Callie are done to keep the peace. I truly don't know how Cal does it.

I find the only spot at the bar with just enough space for me to slide into between two occupied stools. Patiently waiting for the bartender to notice me, I start absentmindedly playing with a coaster in front of me.

"What did that poor coaster do to you?" A gentleman to my left asks me.

I glance down at the coaster to see I have rubbed the paper off on a corner of it. "Just an innocent bystander. Wrong place at the wrong time situation," I say.

"Does it have anything to do with the guy at your table that looks like he has a whole tree shoved up his ass and not just a single stick?"

I glance back and study Trevor for a second and then look at the guy to my left. "I think that is the best description that could be given for Trevor. And yes."

"Need a temporary fake boyfriend?" The guy asks.

I shake my head but before I can get the word "no" out, Brad comes running up to my side and punches the guy sitting on the barstool that I was talking to. I whip around and push Brad back.

"What the fuck, Brad?" I ask him. I turn to the guy on the barstool. "Are you okay? Oh my gosh. You are bleeding." The bartender notices me finally. "Get me the first aid kit. I'm a nurse."

I grab the stranger's face and turn it to get a better look.

Brad grabs my wrists and pulls my hands away. "It is the least this fucker deserves," Brad spits out, pulling me behind him.

I wiggle out of his hold while the stranger continues watching us.

I see when the moment of recognition of Brad's face registers with the stranger. "Ah. I know what is happening now. Go talk to Sandy. She will tell you everything."

Brad stiffens. "She's dead so I don't think she will be telling me anything."

The stranger grabs his stomach. "What? When?"

Brad shakes his head. "Like I would tell you anything after what you did to her?"

The stranger raises his hands. "I didn't do what you think I did. I know what happened, but not who did it."

The bartender slaps the first aid kit on the bar top, points to Brad and then to the door. "You. Get the fuck out of my bar." The bartender looks at me and points to the stranger. "Fix him up and then you can leave too."

Brad grabs my hand. "Fuck him. Come on. Let's go."

I yank my hand back. "I am going to clean up your mess and then I will meet you out at the truck."

Brad gives me a disapproving look.

I throw a hand on my hip. "Or you can leave, and I will call an Uber."

Brad drops his head and runs a hand roughly through his hair before looking at me again. "Fine, I will be waiting in the truck." He points to the stranger. "If you fucking touch her, I will find a swamp to dump you in."

I push Brad to head to the door and turn back to the stranger. "I am so sorry. I have no idea what all that was about, but I have a feeling you do."

Stranger nods. "Yeah, he thinks I drugged his friend. I didn't. But he thinks I did."

I nod while collecting what I need from the first aid kit to clean his eyebrow. "That could set someone off."

Stranger flinches when I put the alcohol pad to the cut. "Yeah, and had I been the one to drug her, he would have every right to throw me in a swamp."

I lean forward and blow on his eyebrow to dry the alcohol so I can place a couple butterfly strips across it.

He looks up through his lashes. “Is he your boyfriend?”

I place the strips on his eyebrow. “No.”

“He wants to be?”

I look at this observant stranger in front of me. “Yes.”

“I don’t blame him.”

I blush. “I think that punch is affecting your eyesight.”

Stranger places a hand on the outside of mine. “Who do you think I was looking at to even notice the guy with the tree up his ass?”

I shake my head. “Again, I am so sorry for all of this. I hope you have a better night.”

“Tell me your name, and my night will be better.”

“Why would that make your night better?” I ask

“That way when I say my prayers before bed, I can thank God for sending me an angel. I figure that you will get like a gold star next to your name on his list if I mention you by name.”

I laugh. “Charming.”

Stranger shakes his head and throws out his hand to shake. “No, not Charming. Jayden.”

“Quinn,” I respond as I shake his hand.

"Thank you, Nurse Quinn."

I give a single head nod to Jayden before heading to the table to explain what just happened to Callie and let her know that I will see her at the brunch we are having with my dad in the morning. I give Cal a hug and then head to the door. A quick glance over my shoulder tells me that Jayden is still watching me leave so I give him a little wave before walking outside to face Brad who is pacing around his truck.

Without saying a word, I walk up to the truck, open the passenger door, and jump inside, slamming the door behind me. Brad walks around to the passenger side of the truck and opens the door I just slammed. He grabs my legs and turns me so that my feet are dangling outside of the truck. Like a boy looking for comfort, he drops his head in my lap and wraps his arms around my back.

"I am so sorry, Quinnie. I didn't mean to scare you or to upset you. Seeing you with him…it terrified me. What he did to Sandy. She trusted him, met him out here at this bar, and he drugged her. She had the wherewithal to call Reed immediately and he came to get her. Reed found her in that guys arms, barely conscious. Thankfully, he got to her in time. But when I walked off the dance floor and saw him looking at you that way…it scared me. I don't know what I would do if someone did that to you."

I huff out a breath and run a hand through his hair. "I understand why that was triggering." I lift his face, so he has to look me in the eyes. "But, in the future, let's not assault people. I know that I am a badass, but I am not built to break up two grown men fighting over me."

Brad jerks his head back. "Was he hitting on you?"

I grab his cheeks. "Yes, but I didn't mean fighting over me in that sense. I meant in the literal way since you are both ogres compared to me."

Brad kisses my wrist. "Not the time for cute little jokes, Jelly."

I shrug. "Just trying to make sure we are in a better headspace before hitting the road."

Brad looks down. "Did I lose my chance to play Naughty Nurse tonight?"

I laugh. "Absolutely. Naughty Nurse is a reward. Tonight, you are just stuck with plain old me."

Brad kicks the ground. "Damn, guess you will just have to do."

"Now take me home so I can kiss you."

Brad looks around the parking lot before leaning down and kissing my thighs. "Yes, ma'am."

Chapter 10
Brad

The entire ride home, Quinn has been quiet, staring out the passenger window. I can't get a solid read on her mood. Even though she was joking and saying everything was okay at the bar, I can't help but feel like it isn't. That she was just saying that to calm the moment.

After parking, I walk around to open her door, but she jumps out and starts walking into the house before I can even make it halfway around the truck.

"Quinnie."

She puts a finger to my lips as she passes me and continues walking in silence.

I follow her quietly, internally freaking out thinking that I just ruined any chance we had before we ever got a chance to explore what it was that we had going on here. I lock the door behind us when we get inside and watch her walk down the hallway. At the end she turns to look at me and then points to her bedroom before she heads into it. A spark of hope flickers in my chest as I make my way to her room.

Once I step in, I see her sitting on her bed. Her dress is hiked up around her waist, and her beautiful cunt is on full display for me. She holds a finger to her lips, telling me not to talk as I stalk toward her. She holds out a hand to stop me from walking. She points to her knees and then the ground. I immediately fall to my knees. She crooks a finger, motioning for me to crawl to her now, so I do. I crawl to her, my heart pounding so loud that I am sure she can hear it. When I get close enough, she lifts one leg, plants her foot on my chest to stop me, and then stands, her dress falling back into place.

Quinn bends over, mouth against my ear before whispering, "If you ever put me in a position where I have to clean up a mess you created again, the pussy you were just willing to crawl for will become a memory that you will have to dig out of your spank bank on lonely nights. Do you understand?"

I nod my head. "Yes, ma'am."

Quinn stands, walking backwards to the bed before lifting her dress and taking her seat on the edge of the bed again. "Good. Now come and make it up to me."

I continue crawling on my knees to her. I grab her thighs and spread them wider, glancing up to see her watching me intently.

I lean over and kiss the inside of her right thigh. "I am sorry."

I lean to the other side and kiss the inside of her left thigh. "I will never upset you again."

I rub my thumbs up the inside of both of her thighs. "I promise to only make you happy. Stupidly, blissfully, happy."

Her eyes don't leave mine; her breathing is the only giveaway that I am affecting her at all.

My mouth close enough to her soaking cunt that she can feel my breath when I say, "I will always, always make sure that you are safe." I lick up her slit. "That you are taken care of." Another lick. "And that you are satisfied," I say before swirling my tongue against her clit.

Quinn's head falls back as she grips her hands into my hair, scooting closer to the edge of the bed.

With my head still between her thighs, I slide a hand up her stomach, between her breasts, and push her back against the bed. I snake my hands around her legs and toss them over my shoulders before gripping her hips to hold her steady when I pull her further off the edge of the bed. She is trying to squirm to rush her orgasm, but I pull back just enough to let her know that I will let her play the dominatrix all she wants, but at this exact moment, she is at my mercy. When she relaxes against the bed again, I continue eating her out. Moving one thumb to the top of her clit to apply more pressure while I lick, nibble, and suck on it. Her breathing is getting more ragged; I know her orgasm is close. I slide two fingers into her tight cunt, enjoying the moans that slip from her lips when I do.

I start pumping my fingers in and out of her and pinching her clit with my free hand. "I should be recording this so you can see how fucking gorgeous your cunt is when it is dripping with your arousal and my saliva."

Quinn grips my hair tighter and starts moving her hips.

I let go of her clit to give it a quick smack and feel her clench around my fingers.

"You dirty, dirty girl. You like that huh?"

"Do it again, Brad. Do it again. I am so close."

I lean forward, bite her clit, and then pull back to give it three more smacks. Her body goes rigid for a second before relaxing. Her cunt is clenched so tight around my fingers that they might break before she lets out a soft giggle.

I give a quick lick up her pussy before standing.

Quinn sits forward, grabbing for my buttons on my shirt and undoing them. "Are you going to be able to be quiet while you fuck me or should I just give you a blowjob?"

I scoff. "Me be quiet? You are the noisy one."

Quinn grips my pants and pulls them down. "Blow job it is."

Before I have a chance to say anything else, Quinn has my cock in her warm mouth. I am still standing in front of her while she sits on the bed. I reach down and grab her dress, pulling it up, forcing her to pull back from my dick. Seeing her tits fall out and hearing the soft slap they make on her ribs when they fall is one of the most satisfying sounds I have ever heard.

Her hands grip my dick again and she stares up at me. "Are you going to let me continue now?"

I nod down at her and watch her swallow my cock again with a satisfied hum. One hand moving in tandem with her mouth, the other gripping one of my ass cheeks. Every now and then, a tear slides down her cheek, and it just makes me harder. She lets go of my ass long enough to grab my wrist and pull my hand back towards her hair. She looks up at me with a reassuring nod when I wrap her hair around my fist. Then she drops her hand from my cock, both hands going to my ass before nodding again, silently telling me that I have permission to fuck her mouth. I start with a slow thrust, testing what my limits are with her.

When I hit the back of her throat, a couple of more tears slide down, but she keeps eye contact with me.

"If it becomes too much, tap my thighs," I say.

She gives another slight nod with a moan, so I continue my thrusting, picking up speed. She is the first woman that has ever allowed me this kind of blow job freedom, and I would be lying if I said it wasn't a rush. One of her hands leaves my ass to find my balls. When she starts lightly tugging on them, I pick up my thrusting. Saliva is spilling down her mouth and neck, the head of my cock hitting the back of her throat. Between the tugging on my nuts and the groans she is making sending the perfect vibration down my shaft, I feel my balls draw up.

"I am about to cum," I say quickly.

Quinn pulls her mouth off me, grips my cock, jerking it just right, while slapping my cock against her tongue with her mouth open. The sight alone was all I needed. I cum so hard, I see it shoot straight to the back of her throat, some leaking out the side of her mouth while she swallows what she can.

I fall on the bed beside her. "Are you going to kick me out now or do I get to cuddle with you tonight?"

She rolls over to look over my naked body. "My dad is coming over to get me in the morning. We are meeting Callie for brunch. Do you want to risk being caught?"

I sit up. "Why do you have to bring up your dad every time I am naked? You are going to give me a permanent innie if you keep that up."

Quinn laughs and scoots up to get under her covers. "Goodnight, Pookie."

I lean over and give her a long, lingering kiss. "Goodnight, Jelly."

Chapter 11
Quinn

I am woken up by a series of soft knocks on my bedroom door. I tug my blanket up higher. “Come in.”

Lola peeks her head into the door holding a brush and two colorful scrunchies.

“Need some help with your hair again?” I ask her..

She gives a slight nod.

“Lola, where are you? I need to do your hair before we can go get our breakfast milkshakes,” Brad says from the hallway before noticing Lola standing in my doorway. “Jelly, good morning,” he says, staring at my blanket that is clutched to my chest.

“Why don’t you two give me a second to throw on a robe and I will be right out to do your hair.”

Lola tips a corner of her lip and walks towards the living room.

Brad takes her place in my doorway. “Just one little peek.”

I drop my blanket and stand, walking to the chair in the corner of the room. I look back over my shoulder and see Brad nearly drooling. I laugh, grabbing my robe and throwing it over me. "Did you need something?" I ask him.

Brad grabs my ass. "You. Your hand… in marriage…."

I shake my head. "One day, I will say yes and surprise you."

"It will be the best day of my pathetic life, I promise."

I walk into the living room and plop down on the loveseat. Dropping a pillow on the floor in front of me, I pat the pillow for Lola to come sit on. I finish one braid when I hear my phone ringing in my room.

"Give me a second, Little One." I stand and run towards my room but my phone stops ringing before I find it. In all of last night's glory, my phone found its way under my bed. Unlocking the screen, I see the missed call was from Callie, so I call her back.

"Hey babe. You called?"

Callie sniffles. "Yeah, I am going to have to cancel on today. I am not feeling great."

"Oh no. Need me to bring you anything? Soup? Carbs? Coffee?"

"No, I don't need anything. But, um, I probably won't be at school on Monday either. Do you think you are ready to handle it alone?" She asks me.

I bite my lip before answering, "Yeah, I am sure I can, and I will text you if I have any questions that someone at the school can't help me with."

"Sounds good. Tell your dad that I am so sorry and we will reschedule," she says softly.

"Yeah, he will understand. Are you sure you don't need anything?" I ask.

"No, I will get through this. Thank you though."

"Call me if you change your mind, I am here if you need me."

Callie lets out a soft sob. "I know you are. Love you."

"Love you, too."

I stroll back into the living room to find Brad trying to braid the other side of Lola's hair. I walk over to the loveseat, give him a tap, and take my spot back.

"Everything okay?" Brad asks, making his way to the kitchen.

I shake my head. "I don't know. Callie just called and cancelled, says she is sick." I look up at Brad. "But I just, I don't know. She was crying. I asked her if she wanted me to come over and she said no. I just…I just have this feeling in my gut that something is…off."

Brad brings me a coffee and sets it on the table beside me. "Avery and Cal are super close. Plant the seed of doubt with her, she will feel obligated to check in with Cal, Cal will feel obligated to go check on Callie, and in a roundabout way, you will get an answer about your gut feeling."

I finish Lola's braid. "Deviously clever. I will bring it up at brunch. Do you two want to join us?"

Lola nods her head.

Brad shrugs. "I guess we will. I'll text Reed and let him know."

"Where is he at this early on a Sunday?"

"No idea, he just woke me up this morning saying he had to run somewhere."

I take a sip of my coffee. "Alrighty then, let me go throw some clothes on and we can walk over to Dad and Avery's place. Want to see the cats?" I ask Lola.

She gives me a nod and then points to her pajamas and bedroom.

"Yeah, you go change too. Shall we wear dresses?" I ask her.

She gives me a deeper nod with a smile before running off to her room.

I stand to head to my own room but am stopped by Brad grabbing my stomach and pulling me back against his chest. His hand sliding down the silk of my robe and stopping between my legs, gripping me tightly. "Please don't wear any panties with whatever dress you pick. I want easy access for when I bend you over the couch for a quickie during Lola's nap today."

I put my hand over his and begin rubbing myself with his hand before whispering, "I'll consider your request."

Brad's head falls to my own. I remove his hand, reach into my robe, run my finger through my drenched slit, and then place my finger in front of his mouth. He leans forward, licking my finger clean before smacking my ass. *I am definitely not going to wear panties now.*

******

The seed was planted at brunch. Avery called Cal on the spot when we mentioned who all was there. With Lola at the table with us, we tried speaking in code about what happened to Sandy with Jayden, but we all just kept confusing each other, so dad took Lola to the donut shop next door for her morning milkshake.

"I don't think she ever told Reed about it. She didn't want to worry him, and she never mentioned whether she told him or if she called the detective on the card Jayden gave her. I was so caught up in my own shit with your dad that I never even thought to ask her," Avery says solemnly.

Brad pats her shoulder. "We couldn't have known, Davey. Was the card in her stuff?"

Avery nods. "Yeah, it is in a box still at my house. We are planning a trip to go see Memaw and take the last of her things out there. I can go through the box and find it though. I'll call and at least see if she ever reached out to the detective. No harm in knowing. So, what did Jayden say to you?"

I shrug. "Just that he didn't do it."

Brad leans back, crossing his arm. "I'm sure that isn't all he said."

I don't know why the way Brad said that just got under my skin, but it did. "You are right, that isn't all he said. He also asked if I was single and that when he said his prayers last night, he would thank God for sending an angel to fix him up after someone who assumed something about him punched him in the eye."

Brad's whole body goes tense.

Avery's eyes bounce between me and Brad before a smirk lifts her lips.

I take a sip of my mimosa and look toward the door to see my dad and Lola walking back in. "Chat's over," I say cocking my head towards where they just walked in.

Luckily, our food arrived at the same time that Dad and Lola made it back to the table to fill the awkward silence.

******

Lola fell asleep on the couch watching a princess movie and Brad carried her off to her room. I am pacing the living room, not quite ready to talk with Brad. I don't know why I felt the need to throw it in his face that Jayden was hitting on me. It isn't like it matters but something about his attitude toward the guy bothers me. Even after Avery stated that Sandy felt he was innocent. It just set me on edge.

"Are we going to talk about it or just let it fester?" Brad asks as he strolls into the living room.

I stop to face him. "I don't know. I don't know why it irritated me when you said that. But it did. I am trying to figure out how to verbalize what about it triggered me."

Brad stops to stand in front of me. "I don't like the guy; I will never like the guy. He may be innocent, but it won't change my mind about him. He should have kept a better eye on Sandy when she went up there to see him. He should have kept her safe. She should never have been drugged while she was with him. You may not see him the way that I do, and that is understandable because you weren't here for it, nor did you know Sandy. He is still guilty in my eyes."

I take in Brad's point of view and nod. "I understand where you are coming from, and you are right. I don't have the right to make judgement either way. I am sorry."

Brad bends down and kisses me. "Bend over and make it up to me."

I let out a soft chuckle, place my hands on the back of the couch, and lean forward.

Brad drops to his knees behind me and pulls my dress up my thigh on one side, kissing up my leg. "Glad to see you listened to my plea earlier," he growls out.

I look down at him.

He softly bites into my thigh before standing behind me. I hear him unbuttoning his pants and hear the rip of the condom package. One of his hands snakes back up my dress, gripping my hip while the other one goes to my hair. He wraps my hair around his fist before giving it a tug that rides the line of pain and pleasure. "The next time any man hits on you, I want you to remember who this pussy belongs to."

I look over my shoulder. "It belongs to me."

Brad pulls tighter on my hair and thrusts himself inside of me.

I gasp.

"You are mistaken, Quinnie. This…." his hand moves around to cup my cunt, spreading me wider as he growls, "is mine." His palm pushing against my clit every time he thrusts into me. "No other man will ever fuck you like I do, and your pussy knows it."

His hand slides up to where his fingers are rubbing either side of my clit. "Fuck, Brad."

His hand in my hair moves to my neck and pulls me back against him. "Shhhh, Quinnie. If you wake Lola up, you don't get to cum."

I bite down on my lower lip.

Brad lifts one of my legs and rests my ankle on the back of the couch. This new angle allowing him to hit my g-spot. Within seconds, I am shaking, his balls slapping against my clit sends me spiraling. Brad picks up his pace, seconds later he is groaning and falling against my back.

"Are you done being mad at me?" he asks.

I can't form any words, so I just nod and then lower my leg. Before my foot even hits the floor, we hear the front door handle jiggling.

"Shit," Brad whispers out, pulling my dress back into place and rushing down the hall.

I sit on the couch and pull my phone out just as Reed walks in.

"That was weird. The front door is never locked," Reed says, walking inside and putting his keys in the bowl by the door.

I shrug. "I probably locked it out of habit and didn't even realize it. I'm sorry."

Reed shakes his head. "Don't be. Lola taking a nap?"

I nod. "Yeah, she has been out for about half an hour now."

Reed kicks his shoes off. "Nice. I am going to try to get a small nap in myself. Someone was moaning in their sleep last night… I could hear it all the way in my room," he says, giving me a knowing look.

I can only blush in response.

Reed turns to head to his room. "Don't let your dad find out. I actually like Brad."

All I can do is nod.

Chapter 12
Brad

Ron is standing on the stage, Broadway song playing as he breathes in for his opening lyrics when I feel a hand run down my back.

"Surprised to see you here, Brad," Tiffany says.

My nose burns from the stench of her cheap, vodka-soaked breath. "Why would it be a surprise?"

Tiffany shrugs her leathery looking shoulders. "You haven't been coming around as much lately."

I take a sip of my whiskey. "Been watching for me?"

She lays a hand on my forearm. "Well, yes. I thought that…maybe you would want to…"

I turn to check out Ron, mid crescendo, when I see my Jellyfish has walked in and is staring right at Tiffany's hand on my arm. I give Quinn a little smirk before leaning back, forgetting Tiffany's existence all together until Tiffany grabs my cheek and turns my face to see her.

"So? Yes?" she asks me.

I shake my head. "Sorry, what did you say?"

Before Tiffany has a chance to speak again, Quinn drops down on the barstool next to me, pretending not to notice me.

I turn to Tiffany. "Yeah, sure. Look, it was good to see you," I say dismissing her and turning all my attention to my little Jellyfish beside me. "Looking good today, Jelly."

Quinn turns to face me; giving me a long and lingering look up and down my body before shrugging. "Sorry, did you say something?"

I lean down, putting my mouth against her ear and growl out, "Are you wanting to role play as strangers tonight, Jelly? Do you want me to buy you a couple drinks, sweet talk you a little, and then tonight before leaving, fuck you in the parking lot?"

Quinn looks at me over her shoulder. "That what keeps bringing Tiffany back around? Your good old parking lot fuckings?"

"Is that jealousy I hear?" I ask.

Quinn wrinkles her nose. "More like disgust. If you have something that is unresolved," she says nodding towards Tiffany, "resolve it. One way or the other."

I shake my head incredulously. "Nothing to resolve. I want you and only you, Jellyfish. I have had some good old parking lot fuckings, but none with Tiffany. Nor will I ever."

Quinn nods her head with a hum that tells me she doesn't believe me.

"Damn. I will just have to prove that you are all I want." I turn to the bar. "Patsy Fine, get me and Quinnie my set up. I need some liquid courage."

Patsy shakes her head and grabs six shot glasses.

"Brad, it's a school night. We don't need to get drunk tonight," Quinn says.

I kiss her temple. "Hush, hush. We will be fine."

******

I walk into the nurse's office with a large coffee in hand as a peace offering. When Quinn lifts her head from the paperwork she is glaring at, her glare targets in on me.

I extend my hand holding the coffee. "I brought you a cup of 'must forgive Brad' coffee."

Quinn's eyes narrow even more as she grabs the Tylenol bottle on her desk. "Then toss it down the drain and I will go get a normal, no strings attached coffee on my own."

I crouch down beside Quinn's chair. "Please forgive me. I didn't realize how much we drank last night. I mean the first round of three was needed. I couldn't have serenaded you with 'I'll Never Break Your Heart' without it. The other ones, I just… I just lost track of time and was in fun mode I suppose."

Quinn grabs the coffee from my hand and throws a couple of pills in her mouth. "I will think about it. But, one thing that is certain, no more school nights. I can't do this. The health of these kids is way too important for me to feel this way. I nearly gave a kid the wrong medicine earlier because my head was pounding so hard that I could barely read the label."

I nod. "Okay, no more school nights. Done deal if you will forgive me."

Quinn shakes her head and then grimaces from the pain it caused. "Maybe when I feel better."

I stand to leave since I have a class starting soon. "I will take that as a yes. See you after school, Quinnie."

******

After work, Quinn requested that we stop by a store so she could grab some soup for dinner. Her stomach still isn't ready for solid food after last night's alcohol consumption. I leave her in the truck while I run into the grocery store to find the one she wants and to get her some flowers. I am reaching for the sippable soup she requested when I hear my name being loudly whispered behind me.

Turning around to face the women who are obviously talking about me, I come face to face to face with Tiffany and Jessa.

"Ladies," I say with a tip of my head.

Jessa puts a hand to her chest. "I haven't seen you in years. You look amazing. How have you been?"

"I am good. You look great too." I turn around, grab the can of soup in hopes of making it over to the flowers without any followers, but am disappointed to hear a set of high heels and a set of flip flops following behind me. I grab one of the pre-vased sets of flowers and a bear with a little balloon that says "Get Well Soon" on it before heading to a checkout lane.

"Yeah, he is looking way better than he did nearly a decade ago. Back then, I wanted his friend, but Gina got her hooks in him. What a shame. Oh, maybe he is ready to start dating now that Gina offed herself," Jessa says to Tiffany.

There is a person standing between us in the checkout line and that person is the only thing saving Tiffany and Jessa at this moment. I have never believed that a man should lay a hand on a woman in anger before, but this conversation is testing my beliefs. I can feel the blood in my body boiling. I need a shot.

Tiffany shakes her head. "I doubt it. Gina killed his girlfriend…nanny…I don't know what she was at that point. Gina had the woman arrested on false charges and then killed her. It was nuts. But keep your claws away from Brad. I have been trying to butter him up for months now and you showing back up in town won't ruin the progress that I have made."

Jessa tosses back her hair and lets out a laugh. "May the best woman win. Loser buys drinks for a month."

I stand there stunned as the two women shake hands. I change my course and walk over to a self-checkout lane. I typically avoid these because I believe that if we refuse to use the checkouts without a human, they will go back to having actual cashiers or something, but right now, I just want to get the hell out of this store.

I pay for the soup, flowers, and bear with the balloon before speed walking back to the truck. Right as I open the driver's door, a hand reaches out grabbing my arm. I see Quinn start to roll over to face me from the passenger seat that she laid down to nap in while I was in the store.

"Now that I am back in town, we should pick up where we last left off. Still want to show me to that old lifeguard stand?" Jessa asks.

I glance over at Quinn again and see the anger flash in her eyes before she rolls over to face the passenger door again.

I face Jessa and sternly state, "No, I'm good." I get into the seat and attempt to shut the door, but Jessa stops it.

She glances at Quinn before asking, "Is it Tiffany? Because she would be down to join us. I know that is what you wanted before."

Quinn lets out a soft scoff.

I look up at the roof of the truck. "No. Like I said before, I'm good. Goodbye Jessa." I lean over and remove her hand from my door before shutting it and turning towards Quinn.

"Jelly?"

Quinn just puts a hand in the air to silence me.

I let out a groan. "Jelly, it's not what you think. I promise."

Quinn still doesn't say anything and just waves me off with her hand.

I put the flowers in my cupholder, the soup and bear on the top of the console and put the truck in reverse. I know that saying anything right now would be a losing battle.

When we get to the house, I follow Quinn inside like a lost damn puppy. Her stomping into the house, me behind her carrying "forgive me flowers" and an "I'm a dick gift" while following her every step. "Jelly, please. Let me explain."

Quinn whips around. "I don't have the energy today. I want my soup and my bed. I have spent half the day throwing up the alcohol from last night, and the rest of it dehydrated and hung over. Just let me recover before I have to deal with your ghosts of girlfriends past."

I stop in the living room and don't follow her any further. She wants space so I will give it to her for the rest of the day.

Chapter 13
Quinn

After an hour-long power nap, I emerge from my room to have my soup and get this talk with Brad over with but am met by only Reed and Lola at the dinner table.

"Little One, how was your day?" I ask Lola while watching intently for any subtle shrug or smirk to get an idea of whether her day was good or bad.

Lola looks down at her meal and tilts her head to one side, but it was enough to show me the slight upward tilt of the corner of her lip.

I nod. "That good huh? I am glad you had a good day, Honey Bunny."

Lola looks up at me at the new nickname I am trying out for her. I make bunny ears with two fingers on one hand and bounce it in the air before shooting her a wink. She makes the peace sign bunny ears like I did and bounces them in the air.

Reed looks between us with a smile. "How was your day, Jack?"

I groan. "I'm already too old to pretend I am twenty-one."

"You are twenty- two. What are you talking about?" Reed laughs out.

I shrug. "That year makes a difference."

Reed shakes his head. "Anytime you go out with Brad, expect to feel awful the next day."

I rub my forehead. "I have learned that lesson. I'm going to go get a pick me up hydration infusion at Cal's. Need me to grab anything on my way back tonight?"

Reed shakes his head. "No, Brad is picking up Lola's juice that I forgot on his way home tonight."

"Oh, I thought he was here."

Reed looks towards Lola and then back at me. "No, he said something about going to see Ron at the Roost."

I bite on my lower lip to remind myself to watch what I say with Lola around. "Okay. Well, I am going to go get reinvigorated," I say with a slap to my forearm. "Want me to braid your hair tomorrow morning, Bunny?"

Lola does the peace sign bunny hop motion again.

"I will see you then," I say to her, mimicking the hand motion.

******

"You are my freaking lifesaver," I screech as I walk into Cal's bungalow.

"You would think that I would be tired of hearing that, but it never gets old. So, Flapjack, what caused you to need my discreet IV services?" Cal asks, guiding me into his kitchen.

"Too much to drink last night."

Cal stiffens. "Were you alone?"

I look at him and shake my head. "No, I was with Brad. You look like you have seen a ghost. Are you okay?"

Cal runs his hand through his hair. "Look, she asked me not to tell anyone, but I feel like you of all people should know. I don't want anything to happen to you too."

I nod to encourage Cal to continue.

Cal lets out a long breath. "Callie was drugged the other night. Someone roofied her."

I drop to the chair behind me. "You are lying. Saturday night?"

Cal nods. "So, after you and Brad left, Trevor had a hissy fit and stormed out. I left shortly after because of my shift I had yesterday. I knew I should have made her leave with me and bring her here, but she'd insisted she was fine and not to worry about her."

I reach out to rub a hand down Cal's arm. "Do not even go there, Cal. You couldn't have forced her to leave with you; she is a grown woman. Do not spiral. What happened after that?"

Cal falls into the chair beside me at the table. "I don't know. Avery called me Sunday morning saying she cancelled on brunch, so I tried calling her a few times and she never answered. A couple of hours later she called me while I was at work and asked if I could meet her down in the parking lot. When I got down there, she was in the same clothes she had been wearing Saturday night. They were all disheveled." Cal lets out a grunting cough. "She was assaulted, Jackie. Someone hurt my sister, and I wasn't there."

I drop to my knees in front of Cal and throw my arms around him in the tightest hug I can manage while his tears start to fall. "I am here. I am here with you."

Cal wraps his arms around me. "Thank you, Flapjack."

The doorbell chiming pulls us from our somber moment of silence.

Cal loosens his hold on me. "Shit. I forgot he was coming. Umm, so you remember the guy Brad punched?"

I nod and follow Cal to the front door. When he swings it open, I am surprised to see Jayden on the other side.

Cal invites Jayden inside. "Jayden, this is Jacqueline. Flapjack, this is Jayden."

I extend my hand out to Jayden. "Yeah, we met the other night. How is your eyebrow looking?" I stand on my tip toes, trying to get a glance at his eyebrow.

Jayden pushes his blonde hair back from his forehead. "This angel worked some magic, and it is already starting to scab. I am hoping I am left with some badass scar to remember her by."

I cock my head to the side. "You mean to remember him by?"

Jayden shakes his head. "No, I mean her. I made sure to mention her by name in my prayers." Jayden gives me a soft smile before turning to Cal. "Am I interrupting? I can come back at another time."

Cal shakes his head. "No, I was just filling Flapjack in on what happened. Jayden's cousin was drugged at the same bar. Sandy as well. When Callie and I went to talk to the detective, we ran into Jayden up there."

Jayden claps Cal on the shoulder. "As soon as I saw Callie, I had a good idea of what happened, so I went to the detective that is over my cousin's case and asked if he could take over Callie's. I am pretty sure it is one guy that is doing this. Unfortunately, with a lot of the bars having the same regular customers, it is taking a while to weed out the ones we know for sure are not drugging people."

I look at Jayden quizzically. "So, are you like an undercover detective or something?"

Jayden laughs. "No, just someone who goes and crowd watches. I know the detectives are overwhelmed and understaffed. I pick a bar that someone has claimed to have been drugged at, go on random but busy nights, and keep notes of people I see. After what happened to my cousin…and Sandy…I realized this problem is bigger than most people can even imagine."

I nod. "Makes sense. Cal, I can survive without your help tonight. You two do what you need to do and keep me updated about things. I will reach out to Callie tomorrow and nonchalantly invite her to do something."

Cal points to the kitchen table. "Get your little ass over to that table and let me stick you. Jayden and I can compare notes and talk about things with you here. Besides, maybe you might remember seeing someone we didn't."

I turn around to head back to the kitchen and take a seat at the head of the table. Jayden sits beside me to my left while Cal rummages around in his fridge, pulling out a beer for Jayden and juice for me.

Jayden taps the table in front of him. "So, you made it home safely Saturday?"

I nod. "I did."

"Good." Jayden points to the bag of saline and the IV start kit on the table. "I just wanted to make sure with all of… this."

I look at everything laid out on the table. "Yeah, I am okay. My dumbass just drank too much last night and dealt with a wicked hangover today."

Jayden nods. "Those suck."

Cal sits down at the table. "You know that with your POTS diagnosis, you can't be willingly dehydrating yourself."

I wave off Cal's concern. "I know. I wasn't thinking last night, and I have paid for it today. I promise. I won't make that mistake again. I have been able to keep it somewhat under control. I mean, the best that I can for a disease that annihilates your body's ability to regulate simple things."

Jayden turns to face me. "POTS?"

I flinch as Cal sticks the IV into my arm. "Yeah, Postural Orthostatic Tachycardia Syndrome. My autonomic nervous system is messed up from a procedure I had. Now my body thinks it is in fight or flight mode when it isn't, my blood likes to drop it like it's hot every time I stand up so I get dizzy, my heart races, and my blood pressure will drop low. I get dehydrated easily and should stop drinking alcohol completely, but I want to try to enjoy one of the few perks of finally being old enough to drink and young enough to survive on less sleep. It's a lifelong disease that affects so much more but that is what I personally deal with the most. It's super annoying and at times embarrassing, but it is what it is."

Jayden nods. "Sounds scary."

Cal finishes hanging the saline on the portable IV pole. "It is. The number of head traumas and broken bones that I have seen come in from a patient that has POTS is astounding."

I wave my hand in the air. "Enough about me and my issues. Let's get back to what happened this weekend. Fill me in."

******

After hanging out at Cal's for a few hours with him and Jayden, my brain is ready to explode with all the information that Jayden told us. The number of women and men that have been roofied in the area is disturbing and terrifying. I really want to run to Callie's and just be with her to support her through this, but Cal said she was adamant that she was not ready to talk about it.

I know that Lola is asleep by now, so I unlock and open the door as quietly as possible but can't stop the startled yelp I let out when I open the door to find Brad sitting on the couch.

"Turn a damn light on, you nearly made my heart stop beating!" I whisper yell at Brad.

He slowly turns to face me, taking me in from head to toe, before standing and walking over to me. "Do you hate me?"

"What?" I ask him, shaking my head. "What are you even talking about right now?"

Brad reaches out his hands and grabs my face. "I can't have you hating me. Anyone else in the world can, but not you."

I grab Brad's wrists. "I think you drank a little too much tonight, Pooks. Let's get you in bed." I start walking Brad toward his room, but he turns and walks toward mine. I close the door behind me while watching him walk to my bed and fall onto it.

With his face in my mattress, he pats the spot next to him. "Come wrap your tentacles around me, make me feel anything other than what I am feeling right now."

I sit down next to him and run my hand through his hair. "And what feeling is that?"

He rolls his head to the side. "Anger. Sadness. Regret. Remorse. You asked me to tell you something no one else knew…Sandy is dead because of me. I introduced Reed to Gina. I dragged him out to go on a double date with me. The girl that was at the grocery store was the one I wanted to go on the date with. She wouldn't go unless I had a date for Gina. I dragged him out that night just like I dragged him to the beach the day we met Sandy. It is all my fault." His arms wrap around my legs, and he pulls his head onto my lap. "You should stay away from me. I will just get you killed, too. My selfishness will kill you, Jellyfish. I almost left you an orphan. Oh my God, your dad almost died because of me, too."

My heart breaks for this gigantic man who is carrying this misplaced guilt. "Pookie, Gina is the only person who holds any blame for what happened to Sandy and my dad." I grab his shoulders and push him to sit up before I straddle his lap and force him to face me. "Look at me when I say this to you, Brad. You are not to blame for anything that someone else did. It is not your fault. Is this why you went out drinking tonight?"

Brad drops his forehead to mine and nods against it.

I lean forward to kiss his cheek. "This is not your cross to carry." I kiss his other cheek. "You are not to blame." I kiss his forehead. "No one believes that it is your fault." I kiss his mouth softly. "And I know that you will never hurt me."

Brad wraps his arms around me, pulling me into his chest with his chin on my forehead, and I feel the soft sobs leak from him before seeing the tear stains on the shoulder of my shirt. I wrap my arms around him tightly, hopefully conveying the honesty in my words through this hug.

I rise up to my knees and crawl to the head of my bed before reaching my hand out for Brad. "Come up here. I can't wrap my tentacles around you when you are so far away."

While he stands to undress down to his boxers, I pull my pants off and reach under my shirt to take my bra off. Tonight isn't about fucking. Tonight is about intimacy. Giving Brad what he needs. Tonight is about erasing as much of his hurt and his pain as I can by just being a sounding board and someone to hold him. Brad crawls between my legs and lays his head on my chest before pulling an oversized throw blanket over us. I wrap my arms around his shoulders and run my hands through his hair until I feel his body get heavy on top of me. When his breathing includes a slight snore to it, I gingerly lean him to his side and curl up behind him. I throw one leg and arm over him before I fall into a fitful sleep dreaming about Callie and other faceless girls.

Chapter 14
Brad

I wake to an unfamiliar alarm and a manicured hand gripping my chest. Looking around the room, I am relieved to see that I am in my Quinnie's room. Most of last night is a blur. I remember sitting at The Roost with Ron, debating which Twilight movie had the better soundtrack after he belted out "A Thousand Years." I remember Patsy shaking her head at me after ordering my seventh…no eighth shot. I remember turning Tiffany's advances down for the millionth time. After that though, it's a bit hazy.

Quinn rolls over with a groan to turn off her phone alarm. "I hear you. I hear you."

"Do you think it knows that you heard it yet?" I chuckle.

Quinn startles. "Fucking A, Brad. You scared the shit out of me. Don't do that," she says, gripping her chest.

I roll over to fully face her. "You literally just pulled your arm off of me. I didn't think I would startle you."

She runs a hand over her face. "It's not you. It's me."

"Jumping straight into the breakup lines before we even get off the bed. Damn," I say, pulling myself to a sitting position.

Quinn waves a hand in the air. "You know the rule. Not before coffee."

I lean down and lay a kiss on her hipbone. "Go shower, I will have your coffee in there before you get out."

"We need to talk about last night."

I kiss her other hipbone. "You know the rule. Not before coffee," I say, mimicking her.

Quinn shakes her head but stands and I enjoy watching her leave her bedroom. Rolling off the bed, I grab my clothes from the foot of the bed and throw my pants on before heading out into the kitchen.

Reed looks up from the pan in front of him on the stove. "Hey, man. Where's the juice?"

I run a hand through my hair. "Shit. I forgot. I am so sorry."

Reed shakes his head. "You have to pull yourself together, dude."

I start making mine and Quinn's coffees. "Yeah, I know. I will take Lola to school today and get her a morning milkshake or smoothie to apologize for forgetting her juice."

Reed nods. "You sure you are good?"

I nod back at him. "Yeah. Golden."

Reed gives me a once over before returning to the eggs in front of him. "If you say so."

******

Quinn told me she wanted to have a talk today but since we had Lola in the truck with us, it had to wait until after dinner. We decided to walk over to the lifeguard stand to talk so that we had privacy from Lola's little ears. I could already tell by Quinn's demeanor today that this talk was not going to be a fun and flirty one.

"I think that we need to dive right into what you said last night and not sugar coat this," Quinn says as she sits down, feet dangling off the edge of the stand.

"Which part of what I said?" I ask. I don't necessarily recall what I said last night.

Quinn glares at me. "The part about how you were so excited that I am pregnant that you want to get married this weekend so that our baby is not born out of wedlock."

I rub a hand down my face and curse myself for being so drunk last night that I don't remember this conversation at all. "Well, obviously, I want to do the right thing for my baby." *What the actual fuck?*

Quinn cocks her head to the side. "You don't remember what you said last night, do you?"

I shake my head. "I won't lie to you. I truly don't."

Quinn nods slowly. "I'm not pregnant. I said that to test your memory but now I know that everything said last night was just drunken words but sober thoughts."

"What do you mean by that?"

Quinn leans back on her hands. "I was a bartender in South Carolina. One thing I learned really quickly is that someone's drunken confessions are their sober thoughts that they keep hidden."

I sit down next to her. "What was my drunken confession?"

Quinn bites her lip before deciding to tell me. "That you think the shootings were your fault."

I look in the opposite direction of Quinn so I can gather my composure. "Just drunken words. Ron's singing really put me in a tragic mood with his Les Mis renditions.

Quinn places a small hand on my arm. "You said you wouldn't lie to me."

Shaking my head, I turn to face Quinn. "Look. I have a lot of things that I regret in life and introducing Reed to Gina is one of them. My anger with myself is not misplaced over that."

Rubbing my arm soothingly, Quinn says, "You are allowed to feel that, but you are not to blame for what Gina did, Brad. You do know that…right?"

I don't agree with her but nod my head to move this conversation along. "Yeah. Like I said, I was just in a weird mood. I will have to tell Ron to lay off the songs that tug at my heart strings for a bit."

Quinn narrows her eyes at me. "I can't help you if you want to stay stagnant."

I put on my smile that usually gets me what I want. "I promise you, Jelly. Last night was a one off. Seeing Jessa put me in a funk."

Quinn nods. "I can understand how it would."

I use this as my opening to take the heat off of me. "Are we going to talk about your emotions around Jessa and Tiffany now?"

Shaking her head, Quinn says, "I know you have past conquests and girlfriends. I am not jealous that you have a past. But I don't want to live in the shadows of them every time we leave the house. I don't mean with a simple run in at the grocery store. I don't want to keep spending our time in the places that they know you will be. There are so many places we can go out to, we don't have to be sitting ducks at the old haunts that they know to expect you at. That is all."

I pull her hand up to my lips, kiss her knuckles, and ask, "Are you saying you want me to ask you out on a real date?"

Quinn lets out a laugh. "You sure are a cocky one."

"I think I have proven that I deserve to be one," I say looking down at my lap.

Quinn shakes her head.

I grab both of her hands. "Quinnie, my Jellyfish, will you go on a date with me Saturday night?"

Quinn studies me for a second. "I have some plans with Callie, but I can squeeze you in afterwards, I suppose."

She tries to hide her indifference behind a smirk, but I know she is more excited than she is letting on. "You just let me know what time works for you."

Quinn nods. "Sounds good."

I look at the door behind me. "So…do you want to…uh…."

"Do I want to go in the lifeguard shack and fuck your brains out?" she asks.

I shrug. "I was going to find a way to word it less offensively for my future wife, but I like your choice of words."

Quinn shakes her head before standing to head inside the lifeguard shack. I jump up and follow her inside. She saunters over to the desk, lifts her long skirt up to her hips and then slides her bare ass on the desk.

I grab a condom from my pocket and drop my pants before I hurriedly shove the cement block against the door. "Take the skirt off."

She raises an eyebrow.

"We have done things your way, Jelly. Give me a chance," I growl out.

Quinn stands and drops her skirt to the ground.

I flick a finger in her direction. "Top too."

She pauses for a brief second before doing as I said.

I point to the desk. "Now, sit."

Without breaking eye contact, she scoots back before lifting herself up on to the desk and spreading her legs wide to give me an unrestricted view of her glistening cunt. I stalk towards her as I lift my shirt over my head. When I am standing in front of her, I open the condom and slowly slide it over my rock-hard dick before I move my hands through her hair, gripping a handful and pull her head back to make sure she sees me when I tell her what I am about to say.

"You are the only woman who I want, who I see, who haunts and graces my dreams." I slide the head of my cock between her slit. "You are the only woman that matters to me." I push an inch into her dripping cunt. "You are the only woman that I want to bare my secrets to." I push in a little further. "You are the only woman that I want to entertain." I push myself all the way into her abruptly and enjoy the way her mouth opens on a soft gasp when I do. "And you are the only woman I want to ever be wrapped around my cock ever again. Only you. Always you."

Quinn's eyes shine with unshed tears and she tries to look away but I pull her hair back again, forcing her to hold eye contact with me while I continue to slowly thrust in and out of her. Wanting her to see, to feel, what I am trying to convey to her. This is not our normal rough, fast, and playful fuck. This is me being raw with her, laying myself out for her like I have never done for any other woman before her.

I wrap my free hand under and around her thigh as I start picking up my pace. She is using one hand to keep herself upright on the desk and the other grips the back of my arm. Our eyes stay locked, getting lost together as our bodies begin to pound against each other.

The lifeguard shack is filled with the sounds of our pants, moans, and bodies slapping together when I feel a cold breeze and hear a shriek from behind me.

I pull Quinn's face to my chest to keep her hidden from whoever is standing behind me before looking over my shoulder to find Avery standing in the doorway.

Without missing a thrust I ask Avery, "Do you want to take a video here or are you going to walk away now?"

I feel Quinn's pussy clench around me as she lets out a muffled moan against my chest. Mental note to ask her about that reaction at a later time.

"You are lucky I am alone right now, Dipshit. But just to warn you, he is meeting me over here for our nightly jog so either shut it up or shut it down," Avery warns before slamming the shack door behind her.

I look down at Quinn. "You heard the woman, better shut it up," I say as I grab her discarded panties, sniff them, and then shove them into her mouth.

Her eyes widen but I can see the smile in them.

I get back into the rhythm I had before Avery's warning slowed me down a little. I couldn't care less if James found out about us, but this isn't how I want him to find out. I am also not ready to stop what I am doing right now.

The moans that Quinn is making around her panties is making it hard for me not to cum instantly, but I'm not ready for this moment to end.

I remove my hand that has been holding her hair this entire time and move it to grip under her jaw. "Jelly, shhhhhh. You are going to cause us to get caught if you can't be quieter."

Her eyes flutter closed as her pussy grips me tighter and another muffled moan escapes.

I look down at her pussy. "God damn, woman. I can't hold off any longer. Not with you squeezing me so tight."

Quinn makes a muffled sound.

"You want me to cum?" I ask her, gripping her jaw a little tighter.

Her head drops back and she pushes harder against me. The muffled moan lasting a little longer. A little louder.

I start pounding into her harder. "This what you want? You want to be heard? You want us to get caught again like this?"

She can barely hold herself up as her orgasm rips through her. Her nails digging into my skin, I can feel blood trickling down my arm as I give a final thrust and release myself into her.

I drop my head to the crook of her neck to catch my breath and feel her moving around under my partial weight. "We will circle back to this voyeurism kink you appear to have another time," I say.

She lets out a soft giggle. "I don't know yet how I feel about this. It was not a kink I knew I had apparently."

I pull my head up and kiss her temple. "Well, we will have to find out at a later date…with a different audience."

Quinn huffs out a laugh and kisses my chest.

Chapter 15
Quinn

I am watching Callie thumb through some paperwork, avoiding making direct eye contact with me. She hasn't spoken five words to me since she got into work today but in her defense, we have had a weirdly busy morning. A lice outbreak among our kinder kids has both of us preparing for a long day on our feet where we both will feel phantom itching because you cannot dig through hair looking for possible lice without your own head itching.

Before our day gets packed, I finally work up the courage to ask her, "Do you need a hug?"

She glances over at me. "Honestly, if you touch me, I will break down crying. Not because I am scared or anything, but because my body will think it's safe and will just allow me to break. I can't do that today."

I nod my head. "I get it. But you know where to turn when you are ready for one, right?"

Callie lets out a soft laugh before schooling her face. "I do. I know I said I want to wait until Saturday to hang out but do you think we can tonight, too? I think I need a little breakdown. Just a small one. I feel like a Coke bottle that has been shaken, I need to let some of this emotion out so I don't explode."

"You got it," I say to her before heading to the line forming outside of our office door.

The rest of the day passes in mostly silence while we look through children's hair side by side. We have a table between us where we are keeping the paperwork, clean combs, and gloves. Callie is facing one way with a kid, and I am facing the opposite to keep the kids from moving their heads to talk to each other. We realized very early on that our thinking it would be quicker with two of us was just a silly fantasy. Once we created this opposite seating arrangement, we found a good rhythm again.

"Lola, would you prefer to have Nurse Quinn look?" Callie asks behind me.

I turn slightly to face Callie and Lola. "Hey, Bunny, give me a second and I will check you out. Go take a seat over there," I say, pointing to a stool in the corner.

I finish with the student in front of me before motioning for Lola to come back and jump in my chair. When I start combing through her hair, I am shocked to see little lice moving around. How have I not noticed the last couple of days that I have done her hair? Probably because it is so second nature now that I don't even have to look to braid her hair the way she likes it every day.

I lean down close to her ear to whisper, "Bunny, we need to treat your hair tonight."

She looks back at me with fear in her eyes.

I pat her shoulder. "Don't worry, we will take care of it. The shampoo stinks a little, but we will handle it."

Lola drops and shakes her head before glancing over to the line of kids waiting at the door. It clicks for me then. It's not the lice that upsets her. It's everyone knowing.

I lean over to Callie. "Do you think you could make it the rest of the day without me?"

Callie glances at the clock. "Yeah, we only have like an hour and a half and one class of kids left. What's up?"

I nod to Lola.

"Gotcha. Yeah, you two go."

"Thank you. I'm going to make this super dramatic so that no one questions her leaving now."

Callie grins. "Make it entertaining. I beg of you."

I start coughing. Not just soft coughing. Loud and dramatic. Arms flailing. I turn my back to the kids at the door who are looking at me before I smile and wink at Lola. She does her little wink blink in return. I turn back to the door and see Brad standing there, his eyes not hiding his concern. I throw my arms up again before tapping Lola and pointing to my purse. She turns and walks over to grab it right as Brad gets to my side.

"Are you okay?!" He asks. "Here, put your arms above your head," he says as he grabs my wrists, lifting my arms over my head, and pulling me to stand abruptly.

The sudden postural change causes my blood to pool to my lower body, reducing the amount of blood pumping to my heart causing my heartbeat to race, forcing my blood pressure to drop drastically, and my vision to go black. *Lovely.* I feel the dizziness hit me hard and know this will be a full faint episode, not just an "if I sit down quick enough it will level out" situation.

I come to in Brad's arms. He is frantically carrying me towards the door that leads to where he parked his truck. I turn my head slightly and see Lola trailing behind him with my purse over her tiny shoulder. Her face is pale.

"Barb! Get the door!" Brad rushes out.

"What is going on?" Barbara asks.

I am still a little dizzy and can't force the words out of my mouth that I will be fine.

"She fainted. We are taking her to the ER. Get the door for me!" Brad says in a panic.

I hear the door open and feel the warm air and sun hit my face.

I am nearly able to think again when I hear the truck door open before Brad lays me across the front seat.

"Get our girl taken care of," Barbara says.

"I will. Come on Lola, let's go."

I hear the sound of the seat belt being buckled behind me and then the door shut.

I slide my hand between the seat and the door so I can grab Lola's foot. I feel her slight jerk before she relaxes.

"I'm okay, Bunny," I get out hoarsely.

Brad flings his door open before jumping into the driver's seat. I reach over with my other hand and grab his arm.

He lets out a relieved breath when he looks at me for a split second before concern takes over again.

"I am okay. We don't have to go to the ER."

Brad huffs out, "The hell you don't. You just fainted Quinnie. You are going to the ER."

I shake my head. "I truly don't. I promise. Just take us home. I will be just fine."

Brad glares at me.

"I just got carried away with my fake coughing. We need to hit a pharmacy to grab lice treatment and then head home."

Brad looks between me and Lola before leaning over towards me. "You swear that you will be fine?" he whispers.

I run a hand over his sweet face. "I pinky promise."

Two hours later, Callie and I are hanging out in the bathroom with Lola between us while we comb out her freshly lice treated and washed hair.

"I think I had lice nine times as a kid and twice as an adult," Callie says.

Lola's eyes meet hers in the mirror showing her surprise.

I nod. "I think I had lice four times and three of them were because of you." I shoulder bump Callie and we both let out a giggle.

Lola eyes dart between us in the reflection of the mirror.

Callie sections off another chunk of Lola's hair. "I can't help it. If it wasn't me bringing it home, it was Cal. Between us and our friends, I am sure we were included in every lice outbreak at our elementary school."

I drop the section of hair I am working on. "I need a pick me up. I'm going to make an iced coffee. Want one?" I ask Callie.

She nods.

"Want a milk?" I ask Lola.

She scrunches her nose.

"A juice?"

Lola nods her head once.

I'm mixing instant espresso and Nesquik powder with some hot water when Brad comes up behind me, wrapping his arms around my stomach.

"You know we have an espresso machine."

I turn in his arms. "Yes, but I hate cleaning that dang thing. This is just simpler. Will you grab the milk and sweet cold foam from the fridge?"

I turn back to making my drink.

"Are you sure that you are okay from earlier?" he asks me.

I nod. "Yep, just a mix of the fake coughing and then standing too fast. I will be fine. I swear it."

Brad glances around before leaning in and kissing my cheek. "If you say so, Jelly."

I reach back and pat his thigh. "I do."

Grabbing our drinks, I head back into the bathroom to finish our task at hand.

******

Callie and I are walking across the shoreline, waves lapping at our feet. "I don't know where to start or which part of this story will make me feel better so…is it okay if I just blurt out what I need to before you ask any questions?" Callie asks me.

I squeeze her hand. "However you need to do this."

Callie takes a deep breath and nods her head. "Trevor threw a fit about me dancing with Brad. When he left, I didn't even feel bad about it. I was actually relieved that he left the bar. I was just kind of…over dealing with his negativity. It is so heavy. Cal, Josh, and myself even celebrated his departure with two rounds of shots, nearly back-to-back. I remember that Cal's phone went off and he left. I danced a few dances with some strangers, most of them old enough to have been one of Blanche's men on The Golden Girls." Callie pauses, focusing on a seashell in front of us. "I remember having at least one more shot after that and then my memory goes hazy. It was like bits and pieces. I remember excusing myself to the bathroom and then it's like…blinks of memories. Being carried-blink. A wooden eagle on the wall above a door-blink. Feeling a scar on the guy's hand when I wrapped my fingers around his thumb to pull his hand away from me-blink. Saying no-blink. Puking-blink. Being moved-blink. Waking up on a park bench with my purse under my head like a pillow and a blue blanket with maroon flowers on top of me."

I squeeze her hand tighter.

She kicks up a chunk of sand and chokes out, "Luckily my phone still had some battery life left, so I tried calling Trevor, but he didn't answer. I got an Uber and that's when I called you to cancel our plans." She holds up a hand. "And don't even start on why I didn't have you pick me up. I was not thinking straight, and I guess…I guess I was trying to come to grips with everything." She shakes her head. "Anyway, when I got home, Trevor was sitting on the couch. He immediately accused me of cheating on him and started berating me. When I told him what happened, he told me I was making up a story to cover my ass for being caught." A soft gasping sob rips out of Callie. "Can you believe that little dick mother fucker?! Anyway. When I realized that there was no point in expecting him to help me, I grabbed my keys and drove over to Cal's hospital. I sat there for about an hour before I finally worked up the nerve to call him."

I can feel that her emotions are getting bigger and this story is about to be harder for her to relay so I lead us to higher sand where we can sit down for what is coming next.

"The exam proved what I already knew. He used protection, but they still gave me a bunch of pills to take, and I have an appointment for a follow up scheduled."

Callie pauses to look around us. After a few minutes I clear my throat, preparing to break the silence but she begins talking again.

"I never would have believed that one night would change every aspect of my life. I walked into that bar as an engaged woman, excited for a new adventure in life and celebrating what I thought was going to be the start of my life finally beginning. I mean, I love it here, but I feel like life has just been stagnant, like I'm just going through the motions. I left that bar as a victim. I am now a single woman, terrified to go anywhere alone. I moved in with Cal and am going to take a break from working all together for a little bit. At least until I can get back to a good headspace. Just going in to work today had me crying in my car all the way in. Trevor will leave Saturday and I will be relieved when he does. I keep seeing the disgust on his face when I walked in the front door and it just made me feel even worse than I already did. It made me feel so…dirty."

I wipe away the tear that is falling down her cheek closest to me. "You are not dirty, Callie."

She sniffles and wipes the back of her hand under her nose. "I know that. I mean, the logical side of my brain knows that. I can't help but wonder about all of the 'what ifs' though. What if I left the bar with Trevor? What if I left the bar when Cal did? What if the guy did worse to me? What if I didn't get to wake up on that park bench?"

I can't stop the sob that escapes from me on that last "what if." I wrap both of my arms around Callie and squeeze her body so tightly that it's possible I left bruises behind. "You are here, Callie. You are here with me. With Cal. The 'what ifs' do not matter. Do you hear me?"

She nods against my neck before patting me and I pull away.

She takes a deep breath with a long exhale. "I think I have skimmed enough that I won't explode. Can that be all for tonight?"

I nod. "Absolutely."

We start walking back the way we came, quiet this time. Appreciating the silent comradery we have between us.

Chapter 16
Brad

I watch from the window as Quinn hugs Callie before she leaves. Quinn stands there for a few minutes watching Callie's taillights fade out of sight. When she walks back into the house, I force myself to stay seated because I can see that her eyes are red-rimmed. I want to comfort her. To make sure that she is alright. But glancing over at Reed, who is staring at me, I know that sitting here is the correct choice right now. I hear the shower in mine and Quinn's bathroom turn on and lean back on the couch.

After fifty minutes has passed, I glance down to see Lola is fast asleep against Reed's side. I hitch my thumb over my shoulder. "I am going to go make sure she is okay. Between the fainting episode and Callie, I just want to check."

Reed huffs out a laugh. "Don't make excuses on my account."

I don't even waste time responding to him. Standing as swiftly as possible so I don't wake up Lola, I stretch out before heading to the bathroom. Nothing could have prepared me for what I saw when I walked in.

I open the shower door and step in fully clothed to wrap my arms around Quinn who is trembling and naked, sitting on the shower floor while the cold water pounds down on her. I glance up to see that the water is on a hotter setting, but the hot water ran out. I jump up to grab every towel in our bathroom, stripping off my wet clothes, and using one for myself while wrapping her in the rest of them before lifting her and carrying her to my room.

She points a shaky finger towards her bedroom.

I kiss her temple. "I need to get you warm, Jelly. I have a thicker blanket, and a million extras thanks to my sisters and their knitting phases."

She relaxes against me. When we make it to my bed, I pull back the covers and sit her on the side of the bed while I take one of the towels and wrap her hair up in it to help it dry. One great thing about living most of my life in a home with two sisters, I know a little bit about after-shower hair care. After I get her body a little warmer, I will switch this towel out for one that is dry. When I have the towel secure, I drop my towel, scoop her back up, and crawl across my bed on my knees. Once I get to the middle of my king-sized bed, I gently lay her down and wrap myself around her naked body before pulling my comforter over us.

In a shaky voice she says, "I need you, Pooks. I need you."

She rolls over to face me, her cold body eating up my warmth, her freezing hands cupping my face.

"Jelly…" I try to protest but she cuts me off with a kiss.

She pulls back and shakes her head. "No, you don't understand. I NEED YOU. I need to feel you, inside of me. On me. Around me. I need to feel something and I want it… no… need it to be you."

She brings her lips back to mine, kissing me softly, deeply. One of her slightly warmer hands trails down my body until she gets to my shaft that has already sprung to life. She grips my cock, lifts a leg over mine, and guides me to her waiting pussy. Already dripping wet for me.

"Let me go grab a condom," I say softly.

Quinn shakes her head slightly. "I'm on birth control and I'm clean. I don't want to feel anything but you."

I let out a soft groan. "I'm clean. I'm worried, though, that you will regret this."

Quinn rocks forward causing me to disappear inside her, her eyes locked on mine. "I want… need to feel you, Brad."

I push forward so that I am deeper inside her and allow my mind to relax when I see her features soften as she starts rocking against me.

This is soft, sweet, and slow. We are not chasing pleasure, just enveloping each other with short, smooth thrusts. Her eyes tell me what her mouth and mind won't or can't-I don't know which.

I feel Quinn's movements getting choppy and I know that means she is close to cumming, so I pull her closer into me to help add more pressure on her clit from my pubic bone. Her silent gasps and gripping hands show me that it was what she needed. I pull my hips back a little more than I had been between thrusts until I feel her clench around me. This is all I needed to allow myself to let go of what little self-control I had and release myself inside her.

Quinn snuggles deeper into my chest, my arms cocooning her upper body while her legs cocoon my lower body. No words are spoken but I notice a change in her breathing a few seconds later. Soft snores escaping with her warm breath against my chest. With my cock still inside her, I allow sleep to take me under as well.

******

I am putting the last of my cleaned and sanitized recorders in their box, my final task before my spring break officially starts, when I hear a soft knock on my classroom door. I turn to find Barbara standing there.

"Callie is taking her leave of absence for the rest of the school year. She just finalized all the paperwork but is still in the nurse's office if you want to go say your 'see-you-later.'"

I slide the box into the cupboard and stand. "Thanks, Barb. I was just finishing up so I will head over there. I figured you would be relieved that she will at least be returning next year."

Barbara looks down at the floor, speaking barely above a whisper, "I see the shell of my Callie. She hasn't told me what happened and she is trying to be strong, but my heart knows." Barbara lifts her gaze to mine. "My heart knows that hers is shattered and I don't know how to heal her. She looks just like you did a few months ago."

I reach out and grab Barbara's hand to give it a squeeze.

Barbara pats the back of my hand. "I can see that you are healing, my child. Slowly, but your eyes show me. I hope I can see that shift in Callie someday, bring my girl's happy eyes back to me."

I pull Barbara in for a hug. "We will see it again. It will just take some time. Callie is a strong woman, and she has all of us. She knows that." I grab Barbara's face to make sure she is looking at me when I say, "And she knows that you are a safe place for her to go, a second mother to turn to if she needs to. You make all of us feel loved and safe. We notice."

Barbara lets out a soft huff and smacks my arm. "Don't make me cry, sugar. Get to the nurse's office or I will make you listen to my rambling about my love for all of you."

With a pat on Barbara's shoulder, I grab my keys and head to the nurse's office. I can faintly hear Quinn and Callie talking so I stay in the hallway to give them some privacy.

"So, brunch Saturday with your dad and then some retail therapy? I want to replace every piece of my wardrobe that Trevor picked out," Callie says, making her way out of the nurse's office.

Quinn makes it to the hallway first and gives me a quick smile before turning her attention back to Callie. "I don't blame you! Yeah, how does ten sound? Dad mentioned having some coffee date with Avery planned but will meet us as soon as they are done. Want it to just be Dad, or is it cool if Avery joins us?"

Callie walks out of the room, nods at me and says, "Avery can come. Cal is always going on and on about their fun adventures and I haven't seen her since our spring break bonfire last year. God, that was a year ago! Can you believe that, Brad?"

I shake my head. "No, it's crazy to think it has been a year since then."

My brain replays the events of that day. Sandy walking into their house after her first actual day of work, opting to stay home rather than joining me and Avery at the bonfire. I wish she would have gone with us. Maybe things would have been different. Maybe she would have met someone that night that kept her off of Gina's radar. The what ifs sour my mood.

"Quinn, are you ready? I told Ron that I would help him put some handrails up on his front steps this weekend, so I need to run to the hardware store tonight to get what I need."

Quinn gives me a nod and then leans over to hug Callie. "See you tomorrow. Love you."

I pat Callie on the head. "Yeah, see you around. You know where to find us if you need us."

Callie smacks my hand away. "You know I will only have the chance to annoy you for a week. Once Jackie-O gets her place next weekend, I will be annoying her and her only," Callie says with an angelic grin on her face.

The reminder that Quinn living with me is coming to an end shortly sours my mood even further.

"Alright, let's hit the road," I say, grabbing Quinn's hand and leading us towards the exit.

Reed picked Lola up at lunch to head out to Betty's for spring break, so I need to take advantage of having no one there to interrupt us this week before she moves into her new place. Ron picked the worst weekend to need this project done but his fall last weekend scared him and to be totally honest, this is one of the many aids he truly needs. While I am at his place, I plan to make a list of all the rest of the things I think he needs to help make his home a little safer for him.

Chapter 17
Quinn

I pass Callie her mimosa. "No, the sex is off the charts amazing."

Callie giggles. "I will never be able to look at B the same. I mean, I figured he would either be extremely boring in bed or a complete freak in the sheets that he just hides well. He carries himself with that 'I'm a shy but cocky' type that you can just never be sure of. Ya know?"

I take a sip of my mimosa. "Well, consider your days of wondering over. I can confirm that he is talented on every end of the sextrum and I feel like I still have more to experience from him."

"There's your dad, so unless we want this brunch to get awkward, let's table this conversation until later."

I look toward Callie. "Avery already knows, she kind of caught us…Dad doesn't though."

Callie chokes on the sip she just took as Dad and Avery make it to the table.

Dad rushes around to her and pats her back. "You okay, Callico?"

The first genuine smile I have seen all week spreads across Callie's face at my dad's use of her old nickname he called her when we were growing up.

Callie pats his arm. "I'm okay. Just went down the wrong way. You know how unforgiving champagne is."

My dad leans down and gives her a fatherly hug. "I was hoping to catch you before you left Brad's the other day, but those damn cats ran off with one of my shoes again and I had to fight Cleocatra for it. By the time I had won it back, you were already gone."

Callie waves a hand in the air. "Don't stress it, Papa J. I wasn't great company that day."

Dad moves back to let Avery in to hug Callie. "Ahhhh, yes. The lice outbreak."

Avery leans in for a hug and I hear her whisper, "I am here if you need to talk, babe. Your brother informed me since I am in contact with the same Detective, but James doesn't know."

I watch Callie squeeze Avery closer in response.

After placing our order for brunch, we keep small chat light and flowing until Dad goes into "Dad Mode" as Callie and I always called it. The fatherly advice, ramblings, and life lessons.

"You two be careful walking down the beach! Don't walk alone! The other night, we were on our nightly jog, and some knuckleheads were getting it on in an old lifeguard shack. As if the stability of that old shack wasn't already unsafe to begin with, could you imagine if a kid went by during that?!"

It is my turn to choke on my mimosa. Avery coughs out a laugh. Callie's face goes from confusion to realization and slyly glances my way.

I clear my throat. "Dad, that is not really brunch appropriate."

My dad looks appalled. "It wasn't nightly jog appropriate either, but I still had to hear it." Dad shakes his head. "Hooligans."

Avery smacks Dad's arm. "Honey, I think the pot shouldn't call kettles names, whoever the kettle may have been." Her eyes slowly land on me. "I am sure we have been in plenty of situations where someone didn't want to hear us." Avery winks at me.

Now it's Dad's turn to choke. "Let's change up the direction of this conversation. Callico, what is new in your life? I feel like I am completely in the dark with anything to do with you since Jack left for college. I am sorry about that by the way. I should have kept in contact with you."

Callie clears her throat before responding, "Well, I was engaged but that has ended recently. I moved in with Cal and have decided to take a little sabbatical. A staycation Eat Pray Love if you will."

Dad nods before asking, "What caused the need for a sabbatical?"

Callie clasps her hands in front of her and looks down at them.

Avery places a hand on Dad's arm and gives a barely visible shake of her head.

Dad clears his throat. "Let me make this perfectly clear to all three of you. There is nothing that any of you can do," Dad reaches across the table and lifts Callie's chin up before finishing, "or have done to you that will make me think of or love you any less. Ever." He makes a point to lock eyes with all three of us before continuing. "You three and Lola are, and will always be, the most important girls and women in my life and no matter what. You can come to me without fear of my opinion ever changing. Understand?"

All three of us nod in understanding before Avery breaks the heavy moment. "I had my sabbatical a few months ago. I went to Costa Rica." Her head drops and sadness washes over her for a brief second before she pulls her head back up with a plastered-on smile. "I made some great friends out there. If you want to go, I can put you in contact with them. They will watch over you and they are quite entertaining. Mateo is pretty handsome too," she says with a wink before turning to my dad and patting his arm. "If you like men in their late twenties…which I don't." Avery throws another wink towards me and Callie.

Callie can't hide her grin. I can't either, I suppose.

"I will definitely keep that option open. Thank you, Avery," Callie says just as our food makes it to the table.

******

My outing with Callie went on longer than expected and by the time I arrive home, it's already getting dark. I throw my keys into the bowl by the front door and find a note from Brad.

Jelly

I didn't want to call you and bug you while you and Callie were enjoying an overdue girl's day. I had to come home to grab a couple more tools, but I shouldn't be too long. I will meet you at the Roost to start our date night when I am done. Keep an eye out for me, I'll be the most handsome guy that walks through the doors. Miss me until then.

-Pookie

I shake my head and giggle before heading into my room to change into the dress I bought for tonight. It is short but flowy, showing a decent amount of cleavage, with the thinnest of shoulder straps. I can't wear a bra with it, which I know Brad will appreciate. I find my phone to order an Uber to pick me up before running into the bathroom, pulling my hair up into a messy updo, and throwing on a fresh coat of powder, blush, and gloss.

Checking my phone, I see that the Uber will arrive in less than two minutes, so I grab a protein bar to snack on for the drive over. I should have made time to eat something. Not like Brad wouldn't be entertained if I were to show up a little later.

When I walk into the Roost, I head straight over to the bar to find Patsy but am greeted by a younger woman instead.

"Hey, welcome to Nightengale's Roost. What can I get you?"

I look around one more time. "Hi. Is Patsy working tonight?"

The woman behind the bar shakes her head. "No, she won't be in tonight. I'm Raven, I will be taking care of you tonight. What can I start you off with?"

I look around at the whiskey selection. "I'll have a shot of Makers and an Ultra." I notice a couple of seats at the edge of the bar are open so I point to them and say, "I will be right down there."

Raven gives me a salute. "Got it. I will bring them right over."

I settle into my seat and shoot a text off to Brad letting him know that I am here and that I am sitting at the bar top.

I lose track of time watching the rotating singers tonight. From the adorable couple perfectly singing "Suddenly Seymour," to the couple bringing some old school country to the table, followed by a guy attempting to rap some song but just screaming into the microphone about how he doesn't know this version of the song causing my head to start pounding.

I look at my phone to see I have already been here for an hour now and try to call Brad to find out where he is but get no answer. I wave down the bartender and order another beer when I feel a hand land on my shoulder.

I turn, excited to see Brad, but am disappointed when I see it is not my Pookie. "Oh, hey Josh."

"Hey Jack! What are you up to tonight?"

I look at my phone again. "Honestly, I think I have been stood up."

Josh rubs the back of his neck. "What dumbass would do that?"

I shrug. "Apparently the one that was supposed to meet me out here."

Josh points behind the bar. "I will be bar backing for about an hour until Devon gets here. If you are still around, maybe we can have a drink together?"

I shrug again. "I am probably going to drink this beer and then head home."

Josh holds his hands up. "Then do one shot with me now. I can have one since I only have an hour left and I am filling in just to help out."

I wave a hand in the air. "Fine. I'll have another shot of Makers."

One more shot turned into a few more shots and beers. After Josh got off, we sat there making friends with nearly every person in the place. Between barstool singing and the whole bar getting into "Gives You Hell" by the All-

American Rejects, the time flew by. It wasn't until my body started feeling heavy that I even noticed that I was drunk.

I excused myself to the bathroom to splash some water on my face and to order an Uber only to find that my phone is dead. I fumble for the lock on the bathroom door and stumble down the hallway before blackness takes over my vision and I fall into someone's arms.

******

When I come to, I look around to see that I am in Cal's living room. With a groan, I roll over on the couch and my hand lands on a head full of hair. I glance down to see a blond-haired head leaning against the couch cushion, looks like he fell asleep sitting next to the couch.

I hear rustling from the kitchen and smell coffee brewing. My heart stops when I hear Callie.

"We need to take her in for a kit immediately. He may have been sloppy with her. Maybe there will be DNA left behind this time."

An uncontrollable shiver runs down my body and the blond-haired man startles.

Jayden's baby blues look so sad when he looks at me. "Hey. I didn't know where you would want to go, so I figured this was a safe bet."

Cal and Callie come running into the living room. Everyone's eyes are on me, watching, like I am a startled animal about to jolt. If I felt more control over my own body right now, they might have been right.

I try to sit up but give up. "What is going on?" I ask.

Cal and Jayden both look toward Callie and she cautiously approaches me.

"Jackie, Jayden found you outside of the Roost last night." She looks down at the floor. "He…um…."

Jayden turns back to me to take over the conversation. "Remember me telling you how I go to bars where someone claimed they had been drugged at, right?"

I give him a nod.

Jayden lets out a huff. "Well, the Roost made it to my list as of last week. I went out there last night after leaving the country bar…and I found you outside."

I rub my head. "What was I doing outside? I don't remember anything about being outside."

Jayden looks down at the ground for a second before bringing his eyes back to mine. "Quinn, I found you on the ground outside. Unconscious." He rubs a hand down his face before whispering out, "Your dress was…uh…well, it was barely on you. Half of it was ripped apart."

I look down and see that my dress is not on me, and I begin to hyperventilate.

Callie puts her hands in the air. "I changed your clothes. When Jayden brought you here, we bagged your dress for evidence, and I put you in one of my baggy shirts and sweats."

"I need a shower," I say as I try to sit up again.

Cal steps closer to the couch. "You can't shower yet, Flapjack. We need to take you in to have a kit done first."

I can't stop the tears that are rolling down my face while I shake my head vigorously. "I can't have his scent on me. I can't have the phantom feeling of his touch left behind on me. I need to wash him off. I need to get clean. I'm not clean. Let me get clean!" My voice is rising higher and higher. I am screaming now. My eyes silently pleading with each of them. "I need to wash him off of me! Please!"

Callie breaks out in a sob and runs over to me, wrapping her arms around me tightly. "I know, Babe! I know! I know that you want to wash him away, but we have to get all the evidence first. I will be with you. I will not leave your side. We will do this together."

I can't stop shaking my head. "I can't do this Callie. I can't."

Callie grips me to her tighter. "We put aside my 'what-ifs' and we will put aside your 'I cant's' because 'what if' didn't happen. We are alive, we are here, and we are together. You can do this. I know it because I did it, and we both know that you have always been so much stronger than me." Callie's hands grab my cheeks and bring our tear-filled eyes level to each other. "You can do this next part. The worst has already happened and now we rise from the pit we were left in."

I grip her wrists and nod. "Let's get this over with so I can shower."

Jayden reaches out both hands to me. "Can I help you to my truck?"

I give him a nod, and he scoops me up into his arms.

"I'm going to make a quick phone call to tell them to expect us," Cal states as he heads back to the kitchen.

Callie walks over beside Jayden and places her hand over mine that are wrapped around Jayden's neck.

Chapter 18
Brad

I hear Ron singing "Good Morning" From Singing In The Rain forcing my brain to realize two things. One- I am at Ron's and it is morning now. Two- I stood Quinn up and am completely fucked. I jump up from the chair I passed out in and scramble around to find my phone and keys. As my luck, or maybe karma, would have it, my phone is dead.

"Running out of here? I was whipping up some eggs benedict for us," Ron states when he enters the living room in nothing but an apron that says "Ask me about my wiener!" with a picture of Jonah Hill dressed as a hot dog from the movie Accepted on it.

"Fucking hell, Ron! Put some clothes on. I have to run but I will check in with you one day this week about that hole on your back porch. Stay off of it until I do. Deal?"

Ron shrugs. "Sure thing," he says before turning and giving me a full view of his bare ass.

I shake my head hoping to wipe that vision from it but am unsuccessful. "I'm going to lock the door behind me," I yell out while jogging to the front door.

On my way home, I swing by the flower shop to get a bouquet that will hopefully bring Quinn's wrath from a ten down to a seven at least. I am surprised when I walk into an empty house. I plug my phone into the charger while I jump in the shower. I come out and check my phone to find three missed calls from Quinn last night and about twenty-five missed calls from Avery this morning. Based off the number of calls, I call Avery back first.

"Hey, is James okay?" I ask when she answers.

She lets out a loud huff. "You better find a way to get into Witness Protection before he leaves this hospital."

I jump into a pair of sweatpants and a tug on a t-shirt. "Why is he at the hospital and why would him being at the hospital lead to me needing to join WITSEC?"

Avery lowers her voice to barely above a whisper, "Because Jackie was drugged and assaulted last night waiting on your dumbass at the Roost. You are lucky that Jackie didn't already tell her father that she was waiting for you, and that she has kept to just saying she was waiting for a loser who stood her up. But I know, Brad. I fucking know. What the fuck were you thinking? Obviously, you weren't."

I can't speak. My chest hurts and my mind is racing but I can't get a single word out to stop Avery's rampage.

"After everything that happened to Sandy, you told Jackie to meet you at a bar and then you never fucking showed? What was so important, Brad? What was more important than meeting her where you said you would? I saw the note you left her when I went to grab her clothes. Why didn't you show up?"

My mouth finally catches up to my brain. "Where is she?"

Avery scoffs. "You really shouldn't come up here."

"Where. The. Fuck. Is. She?" I yell into the phone.

Avery lets out a long exhale. "She is in the emergency department. You can't go in. James and Callie are already back there, and Cal and Jayden are taking turns sitting outside her door to make her feel safer.

"Why the hell is Jayden there?" I ask.

"Because he was the one that found her and took her to Cal and Callies. It's really bad, Brad. He found her half-dressed outside. When I know more, I will fill you in, but I mean it, Brad! You better hide if James ever finds out."

I end the phone call and throw my phone across the room. It bounces off the wall and falls into a pile of clothes that I have sitting in the corner that I had planned to wash today. I start pacing the room. Horrible images running through my head of what could have happened to Quinn last night. What *did* happen to her. I turn around and punch the wall, leaving a first-sized hole behind and look down to see blood running down my knuckle.

I walk to the bathroom to run some water over the cut I just gave myself, pat it dry, and then head into the living room to pace some more until I hear from Avery again.

******

It is nearly midnight when my phone buzzes. I glance at it from where I am sitting and see that it is Avery, so I lunge to answer it.

"Where is she?" I ask.

"She is over here with us," Avery says barely above a whisper. "But do not even think about coming over here tonight. Somehow, James still doesn't know that the 'who' is you."

"I need to see her Avery, she needs me. She needs to know that I am here, and that I am sorry, and that I will take care of her," I rush out.

Avery chokes on her next words, "No, Brad. YOU need that to feel better."

I scoff, "What are you talking about?"

"Give her tonight, okay? I will check in with you tomorrow, but she needs some space to work through what happened."

With a shaky breath I say, "Avery, I didn't mean to. Tell her I am so sorry. Tell her that I am so unbelievably fucking sorry. That I want to be there with her. That I want to hold her and comfort her. That I want to help her through this. Please tell her."

"I will, Brad. I will. When the timing is right, I will. I have to go. I will keep in touch."

I stand and walk into the kitchen, digging through all the cabinets to find all my hidden bottles of liquor. I will need every ounce that I have stashed in this house to get through tonight.

Chapter 19
Quinn

I allowed myself the week to sulk, cry, scream, and rage over what happened to me. I stayed with Dad and Avery for a couple of nights of that and locked myself in a hotel room when I hit the scream and rage part of it. Callie, Cal, and Jayden have checked in on me every single day. Making sure that I have anything that I need and making sure that mentally, I am still staying strong.

I haven't allowed dark thoughts to invade my mind. I know how easy it would be to allow them to take over and drown in them, but I refuse to let myself take that route. As time has progressed, I have small chunks of memories that creep in. When Callie said it was like bits of memory with blinks, she was spot on for how my memories are coming back to me. I remember feeling hot and weird leaving the bathroom. I remember grabbing a hand that was choking me that had a scar on it in the same place that Callie had described. The skin was so dry it felt like it was cracking. I remember feeling the gravel digging into my back. I remember a familiar chlorine smell. Not like a pool smell but something else that I just can't place. I remember a honk, and the guy getting off of me then. I remember being in a vehicle and briefly thinking that I was about to be murdered. I remember hearing female sobs that I now know were Callie's.

I have told Detective Strome everything that I could remember. He informed me that they did find DNA under my fingernails that was sent off, and that he would reach out to me and Callie when he had anything he could share with us.

My dad has been treating me like I am a priceless artifact, walking on eggshells around me, going out of his way to make sure I know where he is in comparison to me at all times so to not startle me. My dad sucked at having the first period and sex talk but has been very open to talk about what happened to me, reminding me that he loves me and that he is here to listen if I want, but that he completely understands if I choose to leave this topic between me, Avery, and Callie.

Avery has made it extremely clear that as far as Brad and I go, she is neutral but sways towards me when the wind blows and she's on that tightrope. I have not asked about him because I don't want to put Avery in a tight spot, but apparently Brad has not offered that same courtesy. When Avery asks if I want her to make up a reason to get my dad out of the house so I can have more private visitors, I have declined. When I do finally speak to Brad, I want to make sure that my emotions aren't a volcano ready to erupt. I want answers, but don't need to lose my train of thought getting lost in the memories of everything that happened that night.

Even though I insisted that I was well enough to help load my stuff from my storage unit to the U-Haul, my dad, Avery, Cal, Callie, and Jayden all refused to let me go and help. I am taking this time to go through my new place and do some dusting while mentally planning the layout of my furniture when I hear a knock at my front door. Assuming that it is the whole gang back with the truck, I swing the door open and have the wind knocked out of me when I see Brad standing on my doorstep holding a large canvas.

"Hey," he says evaluating me from head to toe.

I lean against the door with my arms over my chest. "Hi."

Brad looks down at the canvas in his hands that is facing him. "I wanted to bring you a housewarming gift."

Before he has a chance to say anything else, my dad and Jayden pull up in the U-Haul with Cal, Callie, and Avery behind them in Avery's Jeep.

Brad looks over his shoulder. "Does he know?" he asks me.

I shake my head. "No, I didn't tell him."

Brad does a slow nod. "I deserve his wrath…and yours."

I plaster on a fake smile. "This isn't the time or place for this conversation. I didn't hold up my end of the bargain, so you don't have to hold up yours," I whisper as my dad comes jogging up the walkway.

"Brad, hey man. Long time, no see. You are just in time to help us unload the truck. We could use some more muscles," my dad says, clapping his hands against Brad's shoulders.

"Oh, I was just dropping off a housewarming gift real fast…."

My dad grabs the canvas in Brad's hand. "Glad you found the one you were looking for! I am surprised it hadn't sold yet. Man, that woman is freaking talented." Dad flips the canvas around to show me the painting of a jellyfish. "The woman who painted this also painted the turtle that Avery and I have in our room. She is a badass! She lost two fingers and part of her right hand nearly a decade ago from a medical injury and found her strength in her art. Reed has a painting she did of a manatee too. She truly is inspiring."

"She sounds like it," I say as I grab the canvas and bring it into the house. "Thank you, Brad. You don't have to hang around and help though."

Brad pulls his shoulders back after moving to let Jayden and Cal through with one of my mattresses. "No, I can stay and help."

I hope I am hiding the disappointment I feel from being easy to read on my face. "Okay, then." I turn around and head down the hallway to my room so I can let Cal and Jayden know how I want the furniture to be set up.

Once my boxes labeled "kitchen" were brought in, Avery, Callie, and I congregated in the kitchen to unload them.

"So? Did you ask him what you wanted to know?"Callie asks me in a hushed tone.

I shake my head. "No, he got here maybe a minute before you guys pulled up so there wasn't any time to ask."

Avery pops her head between us. "Want me to make up a scene to get everyone out of here so y'all can talk?"

I huff out a laugh. "No, but I am curious as to what you would come up with to clear everyone out."

Avery waves a hand in the air. "Oh, honey. Let me teach you my ways." Avery clears her throat and then sing-songs, "Guys, can you come here really quick?"

I narrow my eyes at Avery, and she gives me a "calm down" hand wave.

Dad, Cal, Jayden, and Brad all line up in front of Avery in the kitchen.

"Have y'all seen a silver necklace with a V on it?" Avery asks.

All the guys shake their heads.

"Oh, shoot. It must have fallen out at the storage unit. You know the one James. The one Jackie's mom left her with before she high-tailed it on out of y'all's life. The one and only memento she has of her mother's. Oh, I hope we didn't accidently throw it away with those bags that we thought were trash." Avery turns to me to hide her smirk.

Dad scratches his head. "I don't remember seeing a necklace like that ever…come on guys. Let's head back to the storage unit and find it."

I throw my hand out to stop them. "No!" I exclaim, probably louder than I meant to. "I think I kept it with me. In fact, I am nearly positive that I already put it up for safekeeping so that it wouldn't get lost in the move. I am so sorry for forgetting that."

Jayden glances between me and my dad. "Are you sure, Ripper?"

Brad whips his head to Jayden at the use of my nickname he has bestowed upon me.

I nod. "Yep. I am sure. Thanks though. Now get back to work in there. Pizza and beer is for fully put together furniture. Go so I'm not stuck sleeping on my floor tonight," I say as I wave them off.

The guys file out of my kitchen and back down the hallway to the master and guest bedrooms where two are putting together my bed and the other two are putting together Callie's bed. Not officially Callie's bed but she is the only one who will ever be using it so I just consider it hers.

Callie waits until we hear the whir of the drills again before she lets out the laugh she was holding in. "You are a force to be reckoned with, Avery!"

Avery shrugs.

Callie turns to me. "I didn't know your mom left you with a necklace."

I shake my head. "She didn't," I laugh out.

Callie pulls me and Avery into her and the three of us break out in laughter. This is the first time I have laughed in a week, and it feels good.

"Where do you want me to hang the jellyfish?" Dad asks from the hallway.

I peek around the corner to see my dad and Brad standing there waiting for my answer. "Ummm, pick a spot that looks good in the guest room."

Brad's head and shoulders droop.

Dad cocks his head to the side. "You sure you want it in there? It matches the décor in your room better, and it is such a beautiful painting. We could put it in the living room if you want. It would go with your couches too."

"I said the guest room," I say in a clipped tone. I will need to apologize to dad later for being short with him, but I don't want to explain why I want to see that painting as little as humanly possible.

Brad puts a hand on my dad's shoulder. "Let's get it up. I bet it will look best between the bookshelves over the oversized chair."

Dad nods and turns to head back to the guest room. I run my hands over my face, tugging down hard enough to resemble Adam from Beetlejuice with the misshapen face.

Avery comes up behind me and puts her arms around me, laying her head on top of mine. "Don't beat yourself up. He should have listened the first time."

I let out a soft chuckle. "You would think he would have learned that lesson by now."

Avery pats my arms. "You would think so, huh?"

******

"You can do this. You can handle hard things. You can't rule the day, only your attitude. Your glass is half full and will never get full if you don't pour into it. Now get out there and pour, baby, pour." I slap my own ass because Avery swears it seals the deal I am making with myself with my peptalk. Though I find it to be ineffective on making my words manifest, it does make me feel silly for a second which lightens my mood nearly instantly.

I walk out of the bathroom and head into the teacher's lounge to grab a coffee since I want to drink my coffee and not wear it. No matter what anyone says, there is no sturdy cup holder you can attach to a bike that will hold your drink without spilling it unless it is in a bottle and sealed. Not one that I have found at least.

"Nurse Quinn! How was your break?" Barbara asks, running over to give me a hug.

I hug her back, truly enjoying her warmth at my entrance. "It was okay. A lot of resting. How about yours?"

Barbara pulls away, gripping my hand and leading me over to the coffee bar area. "Oh, it was great. I had all of my grands come out for our yearly weeklong 'Granny Getaway.' We used to do it during summer break but now that some of my grands are older, they have sports and friends." She waves her hand in the air. "They are just getting too old to want to be at Granny's all of the time now."

I shuffle around her, fixing my coffee the way that makes it tolerable with powder creamer. "That sounds like such a fun tradition. I wish that I had family around to do that when I was little. It was just me and my dad. Callie and her family became like family for us, and I would join them on their summer vacations every now and then."

Barbara's excitement shifts. "How is our Callie doing?"

I stir the powder creamer some more. "She is doing really well. Why do you ask?"

Barbara puts her hand on mine to stop my mindless stirring. "Sweetie, I am a mama. I see everything. I may not know right away what I am seeing but I always know when one of my littles went through something. Just like now…with you. I can see that you are guarded today. I don't know why yet, but a mama always finds out."

I let out a nervous laugh. "Well, Callie is doing well. She has decided to take a sabbatical to figure out where she wants to be in life without anyone's influence now that her and Trevor have split."

Barbara nods. "I'm glad she dropped that loser. And you? Are you going to tell me or will I find out on my own?"

I pick up a lid for my coffee and turn to head out of the lounge. "Nothing to find out, Barb."

Chapter 20
Brad

Of all the days to wake up on the wrong side of the bed, it had to be today. Somehow, I pulled my charger out of the socket at some point during the night, so my phone died, leaving me with no alarm clock. The first pair of slacks I put on ripped down the crotch when I bent over to pick up Lola to put her in her booster seat in my truck. I hit every single red light on the way here, and then Lola kept grabbing on to anything she could get a grip on, refusing to get out of the truck. I just need to have a cup of coffee to give my morning some sense of stability and I will be okay.

After dropping Lola off in the cafeteria where she likes to sit and read before having to go to class, I rush to the teachers' lounge, hoping to suck down at least half a cup before I have to head to my classroom. I happened to glance down mid step to see that one of my loafers has a hole forming where my toe hits the top of it which keeps me so distracted that I didn't see anyone walking out of the lounge as I turned the corner to walk in.

"Hoooohhhhhhhhhh my gosh!" I yelp out feeling the burn of the hot coffee soak through my shirt.

"I am so sorry! I didn't see you!" Quinn screeches, tugging at my shirt to get the hot spot off of my skin.

I look up at the ceiling to collect myself and keep myself from cussing about how awful this day has been already.

"Let's get you to my office so I can make sure the burns aren't bad," Quinn says.

I can't speak. Still fearing that if I open my mouth the stress of the day will spill out in a string of words that would make a sailor blush, so I just nod.

In her office, I unbutton and pull off my shirt for Quinn to take a look at the area where the coffee hit. "How are you?" I finally get out.

Quinn shrugs. "Here."

"That doesn't sound reassuring," I say softly.

Quinn keeps her eyes on my chest where the worst of the spill was. "This spot looks pretty irritated. Let me put a little burn cream here. I'll get you a couple of ibuprofens, too, to help with the swelling."

I look down at her. "Thank you, Jelly."

Quinn freezes. "I am sorry about your shirt. I might have a baggy t-shirt in one of my saddle bags…."

I shake my head. "I have a spare in my classroom."

Quinn nods and points behind her. "I have some of those paper scrub shirts like they give you at hospitals that you can wear to your classroom so that you don't have to put that one back on."

"Thank you," I say as I watch her gather the ibuprofen, burn cream, and shirt. Her movements are a little less fluid than before. A little less confident. And it is my fault. All my fault.

Quinn comes back over to where I am sitting on her treatment table. "This will just take a second."

When her gloved fingers touch my skin, I get the same electrical jolt that I do when she touches me at home, or in the truck, or in a bed, causing me to gasp.

Quinn looks up through her lashes. "Did that hurt?"

I shake my head. "No. Just stings a little." She doesn't need to know that it is the emotional sting that hurts most. "So, Quinn…I was wondering if we could get together and talk? Alone?" I ask her.

Quinn's hands pause. "I don't think that is a great idea right now."

I place my hand on top of hers. "Please?"

Her eyes dart to my hand and then to my face. With pain in her trembling voice, she says, "I don't think that is a great idea right now, Brad. I already told you that. And will you please remove your hand?"

The magnitude of the damage I have caused hits me like a ton of bricks at her last sentence. "Quinn…."

Quinn raises her hand to stop me before I can continue my sentence. "No, Brad. The first night I met you, you told me I was safe with you, but you lied. You stood me up, leaving me vulnerable. I never would have been at that fucking bar had you not told me you were going to be there. My dumbass should have left when you didn't answer your phone, but I stayed. Like the idiot I am, I stayed thinking you would eventually walk through that door. Instead, you stood me up and I was raped," she whisper yells at me, head shaking frantically with tear lined eyes. After a few seconds, she takes a deep breath, pulls her shoulders back, raises her chin and says, "You will not decide when we talk about what happened. I lost a big part of me that night, and until I am ready to deal with you again, I won't. You will not pressure me into hearing whatever excuses you have for that night."

She places the ibuprofen and paper top in my hand before turning her back to me and walking towards her desk. Waving a hand in the air, she says over her shoulder, "Have the day you deserve, Brad."

I didn't waste time with the paper shirt or the ibuprofen dropping both of them on the table. I darted out of the door with the intention of getting to my truck as fast as humanly possible.

"Hun, are you okay?" Barbara asks as I pass her.

I give her a shaky nod. "Yeah…no…I have to leave. I have to go." I put my hand over my mouth to hold in the screams I want to let rip out of me.

"I'll call in a sub for you, Hun. Get to feeling better," Barbara yells down the hallway behind me.

I wave my free hand over my head in acknowledgement and continue for my truck, praying there are no more run-ins with anyone. I don't think I can hold myself together much longer.

I jump in the truck and haul ass out of the parking lot, making it about four blocks before pulling into the parking lot of an old, abandoned restaurant. Throwing the truck in park, I hit the steering wheel, and let out the guttural scream that I have been holding in. By the time it is out of me, my throat feels raw. I glance at the time. I have three hours before Frank opens his doors. I shoot Reed a text letting him know that I had to leave work early today and that he will have to pick up Lola this afternoon before driving home to grab a bottle of whiskey to hold me over until then.

******

A hand clamping down on my shoulder startles me out of my nap. Nap? I open my eyes slowly to see that I am still at Frank's. A water bottle sitting in front of me and a bag of potato chips beside it.

"Hey, come on man. Let's get you home," Reed says from beside me.

I look up at him quizzically. "What are you doing here?"

Reed nods toward Frank. "He called me letting me know that you needed a ride home."

I look between Reed and Frank. "I'm fine. I need another shot."

Frank shakes his head. "No, you don't. You need to head home, Brad."

I slam my hand down on the bar. "No! I need another shot!"

Reed grabs my arm and starts turning me to face the door. "I think we can have more tomorrow, but for tonight, we need to get home."

I try to pull out of Reed's grasp, but I can't. So, I give in and allow him to usher me out of the bar.

"Reed, stop by the store on the way home and grab me a bottle. Any whiskey will do," I slur as Reed puts me in his passenger seat and buckles me in.

Reed runs around to the driver's door and shakes his head as he buckles his own seatbelt. "All the liquor stores are closed."

I point to the seat behind me. "There is probably a crowbar in there somewhere, we can open a liquor store."

Reed scoffs. "Yeah, we should add breaking and entering as well as theft to our plans for tonight."

I shrug. "Only sounds bad when you say it that way."

The rest of the drive is silent. Reed is quiet when we get home, too. I pass Avery and give her a slight wave as I stumble into my room. Even behind my shut bedroom door, I can hear Avery and Reed in the living room.

"Thank you for coming over on such short notice. She go down for bed okay?"

"Yeah, she was so exhausted that she fell asleep halfway through her bedtime story. How did it go picking him up?"

"Not too bad. He was passed out on the bar top when I got there. Remind me to thank Jayden for the head's up on where he was tonight and for passing your number along to Frank just in case."

"I will pass the message along. I am just glad that Jayden called Cal and not Quinn about finding Brad passed out there. She doesn't need the added stress right now."

"How is Quinn doing? Avery, if she needs anything and I mean anything, let me know and I will help in whatever way I can."

"Honestly, Reed, I don't know how she is doing. Some days she seems to be handling everything as well as can be expected. Other days, she is physically in front of you but vacant in her eyes."

I stagger over to my bed and squeeze a pillow over my ears. I can't hear this. I can't handle this. I can't listen to them talk about how fucked up I am and how I hurt and ruined my Quinnie.

Chapter 21
Quinn
Two months later

"Knock knock! Jackie-O! Are you decent?" Callie yells from my front door.

I walk out of my bedroom in my oversized Almanac Man t-shirt, a pair of flannel pants, and baggy socks that I like to sleep in. "Depends on the occasion," I say, heading towards her.

I spot Callie shutting the door behind her and Jayden. "I brought a gentleman with me."

I stop in the hallway and lean against the wall. "I see that," I say with a smirk.

Jayden walks over to me, wraps an arm around me, and kisses the top of my head. "Technically, I was already here but was going to wait a few more minutes to knock since it's the first day of your summer break."

Callie plops down on my couch. "Yeah, now that it is summer break, what are we going to do? My personal sabbatical ends when school starts back up and that is around the time your new job starts, so we have two months or so to live the lives that teenage us said we would."

I pad over to where Callie is and plop down beside her. "What did our list consist of?"

Callie pulls out a crinkled piece of paper. "Let's take a look. Shall we?"

Jayden huffs out a laugh. "Is that legit a list you guys made when you were teenagers?"

Callie nods proudly. "Yep."

I grab the list from Callie. "One-get drunk on the beach. Two- get drunk at an ocean facing restaurant. Three- get drunk at an ocean facing bar so we can run on the beach afterwards." I look over at Callie. "Did we only want to get drunk?"

Callie grabs the list. "No. Somewhere on here there was one that didn't involve drinking. Where is it?" She scans down the list. "Ah, here it is. Go to the Book Barn."

I grab the list back. "No, Callie. The *Book Bar*. Remember, it was that bar that had book themed drinks. Pretty sure they closed down a few years ago after too many girls were…."

Callie quickly takes the list back from me. "Well, we can't deny that we had a one-track mind as teenagers," Callie says with enthusiasm.

Jayden laughs. "Did you guys not go to parties in high school?"

I shake my head. "No, we were social outcasts. I don't know why you fell into that category Callie, but I know mine was because of my early 2000 inspired emo phase." I look up at Jayden. "In a school full of kids who dressed like they would end up on an episode of Outer Banks; I was dressing like I was going to end up on an album cover for Panic at the Disco or My Chemical Romance."

"No way," he laughs out.

Callie nods. "Yes way! I bet I can find some pics of the epic outfits."

While Callie scrolls through a photo storage app on her phone, I turn my attention back to Jayden. "So, back to your original question, no, we never went drinking in high school."

Jayden shakes his head. "Can't believe my girlfriend was an emo kid."

I smack his arm.

Callie snorts. "Are you really that surprised? I mean, look at her." Callie waves a hand over my pajamas. "Most women our age are into the cutesy matching pajama sets or lingerie. Not a pair of flannel pants with a rock band t-shirt.

I sigh. "You should hear them! Totally worth it."

"Here it is!" Callie turns the phone around to show Jayden pictures of us from high school, and I take this as my cue to make a pot of coffee.

"Let's make a new list," I yell from the kitchen.

I hear Callie and Jayden giggling at one of the photos before Callie responds, "I am so in! Jayden? You in?"

"Hell yeah I am," Jayden says.

"I think we should hold off making the new list until Cal is with us. He may want to get in on the action too," Callie says as she strolls into the kitchen.

Jayden walks in behind her. "Let's all do dinner together tonight and make a new list."

Callie jumps up and down, clapping her hands like a kid. "Yes! I am so excited. Everyone starts thinking of what you want to put on the list!"

******

The list we made consisted of every normal teenager's favorites. It was full of theme parks, water parks, sipping cocktails instead of mocktails on the beach, we even made it down to the Keys for a weekend getaway. We hit Miami for a mid-week adventure where Callie and I finally got the matching finger heart tattoos we always swore we would get.

Today, Callie, Avery, and I are heading to Disney to do something they are calling "Disney Bounding." I didn't even know that was a thing but apparently it is, and it is quite popular. Dressing in everyday outfits inspired by characters from Disney movies or TV shows.

Callie is wearing a green baseball cap, yellow crop top, brown biker shorts, and a pair of tennis shoes. Avery is in a light grey workout tank, a darker grey athletic skirt, light grey tennis shoes, and a cat ear headband. I am in a red baseball cap, a red tank top, with a pair of brown biker shorts that match Callies, an orange overshirt that I left unbuttoned, and an old pair of tennis shoes that I found somewhere deep in my closet. I think we pulled off Gus, Lucifer, and Jaq quite well, if I do say so myself.

While walking around in the Florida heat with a million other people around me does not sound like a fun and relaxing time to me, Callie was so excited for this activity on the list and the guys already said they would not be dressing up for any reason other than Halloween. When I told Avery we were coming, she nearly begged to join us and said we should "drink around the world."

How did I spend my teen years living an hour from here and not know anything about what Callie and Avery were saying? I am so out of the loop, but again, their excitement rubbed off on me. We decided to power walk through the park to hit all of our favorite rides before adding alcohol to the mix, and Cal will be picking us up when we have had enough fun for the day.

"We need to nail down the plans for your dad's birthday. Y'all have any ideas?" Avery asks while we wait in line.

I shrug. "Dad has never been big on parties. Maybe just a small get together?"

Avery shakes her head. "That won't work. We didn't get to do a big bash for his birthday last year because he had to leave on a business trip." Avery's face falls sad for a second before she realizes it and puts her happy face back on. "Anyway, we will celebrate forty-one like its forty this year. We need to do something big."

Callie turns around after we scoot forward a few more steps. "What about a beach bonfire? Where we had that one last year? It's on private property and I can ask the owners if we can do one there again this year. They are usually pretty cool about it as long as the crowd is responsible."

Avery nods. "That would be fun. We could rent a couple of tents to give us some shade during the day. Make it feel like an outdoor resort or glamping feel. Lights strung between them all with a smaller fire in the middle."

Callie's excitement is barely contained. "Oh my gosh! Yes! I know someone who runs a company with something like that. They have the ones that look like canopied beds in a way. Oh, we should get someone to come out and play some music while we all hang out too. I know just who to call!"

I nod along. "I think Dad would really enjoy that. What about food?"

Callie jumps up and down in place like a toddler that has to pee. "I know a chick who does this really cool black stone cooking show. Kind of like at a Japanese restaurant but with this big slab of black stone griddle type thing that she puts over an open flame. It is so fun to watch!"

"Have you ever thought about becoming an event coordinator?" Avery asks Callie.

Callie pauses her excited shuffle and thinks about what Avery just asked her. "No, but I think I could be good at it."

Avery drops down to both of her knees and puts her hands in a praying gesture in front of her. "Callie, will you please take over planning this for me and let me be your first client?"

Callie playfully smacks Avery on the arm. "Get up, woman! You are making people stare."

Avery shakes her head. "Not until you agree."

Callie laughs out. "Fine. Yes. I will plan Papa J's birthday party."

Avery fist pumps the air. "Hell yeah you will."

A mother in front of us cups her child's ear and glares at Avery.

Avery throws her hands up in the air and mouths "sorry" to the mother before turning her back to the woman and giggling. "Whoops. I need to reign in my excitement here. Alright, Callie. Remind me when y'all drop me off to give you a credit card to use for this party and if you enjoy it, I will help you set up a legitimate business plan. We can pull Reed in to help on the financial planning."

Callie nods wistfully. "Yeah, let's see how the birthday party goes before getting too excited."

Chapter 22
Brad

The party looks great. There are four platforms with lounge beds in the sand, fabrics flowing from them with the wind. Lights connecting around the tops of the canopied platforms and weaving over them all to light up the center space between them. A fire pit that resembles a horseshoe shaped metal drum with intricate designs cut out of it sits in the middle of the lounge areas. To the side of the lounge beds there is a stool with a guitar propped up against it. Off to the side about twenty feet, towards the dune, there is a long beer tub with a portable bar set up. A familiar guy stands behind it.

"Josh, good to see you," I say.

Josh nods. "Yeah, good to see you too, man! How awkward is this going to be for you tonight?" Josh laughs out.

I cock my head to the side. "Awkard for me?"

Josh nods his head toward the ramp where I see Quinn, Jayden, Callie, and Cal walking our way. "Yeah, with Quinn dating the guy you punched out the last time we were all together. What was that about anyway?"

I bring my attention back to Josh. "Just a misunderstanding. Can I get a whiskey?"

Josh brushes his hands together before responding, "Sure thing."

"Dude! What happened to your hand?" I ask, pointing to a spot that looks like a scar that won't fully heal.

Josh turns his hand a little to hide the scar. "Cut it on a bottle reaching into a cooler a while back and it keeps getting irritated from the cleaner we use in the bar. That shit dries your skin out so bad which makes healing a bitch."

I glance back over to Quinn and see that she is standing by one of the lounge areas looking at me, so I give her a polite wave.

She acknowledges my wave with the slightest tilt of her chin before focusing her attention back on that jackass, Jayden.

"Don't let Jayden catch you staring at his girl like that. Ever since…well…you know, he is really weird about anyone staring at her," Josh says softly.

I whip my head back in his direction. "His girl?"

Josh cocks his head towards Jayden and Quinn. "Yeah, they have been dating for a couple of months now. How did you not know that?"

I shrug. "I haven't been around much. Just have had a lot going on." I grab my drink and raise it in thanks to Josh before heading to the lounge area.

I don't need to let Josh know that I have spent my entire summer break either in a bar drowning my sorrows, or at home drowning my sorrows. At home is my preference when I can, but Reed has made it very clear that if Lola notices my drinking, they will leave immediately. His house will be finished by the start of the school year and while I would love to have my house to myself so I can sit around and drink freely, I know that having Reed and Lola there is the sliver of humanity holding me back from jumping off the deep end. Forcing me to have a little bit of control when I want to just let the darkness of my mind pull me under.

As if my mind conjured them, Reed and Lola make their way across the ramp at that moment. When Lola sees Quinn, I see the first genuine smile on her that I have seen all summer. Lola lets go of her dad and picks up her pace.

I walk by Quinn and tap her shoulder to get her attention before pointing at Lola.

Quinn takes off instantly towards Lola. "Bunny! Look at how tall you have gotten!"

When Lola makes it to Quinn, she throws her arms up for a hug and Quinn reaches down, picking her up and holding her tightly to her. Lola buries her head in Quinn's neck, and I can see from here the way Lola's little shoulders shake with her silent cries.

Quinn drops to a sitting position right there in the sand, never breaking her hold of Lola, and I watch as Quinn consoles her.

"I wasn't expecting her to be upset when she saw Jack," Reed says as he makes it up to where I am standing.

"I am not surprised. Lola loves her and misses her."

Reed claps my shoulder. "I think we all do. I'm going to get a drink. Keep an eye on her, will ya?"

I nod. "Yeah. Of course."

"Ripper," Jayden yells from behind me, pointing towards the ramp. "Your dad's here."

Quinn's head turns and she murmurs something to Lola that makes Lola's head perk up. Following their glance, I see exactly what it was about. Dragging behind James and Avery are two cats on leashes that look like they want to be anywhere but here.

When James and Avery make it to where I am, I point to the cats. "You brought them to the biggest litter box they will ever have the pleasure of using and that is the appreciation you get."

James lets out a full belly laugh. "You would think they would show a little bit of gratitude, but they hate the leashes and vests more than they like the endless litter box."

"Ungrateful shits," I say before dropping down and petting Lucy Fur and Cleocatra.

Callie claps her hands to get everyone's attention. "Okay, you guys! Let's get this party started! Avery and James, you two are in this tent," Callie says pointing to the tent facing the shorter side of the horseshoe shaped fire pit. "Jackie-O and Jayden, over here. Reed and Brad over there." Callie points to the two tents facing each other on the longer sides of the fire pit. "Cal, process of elimination tells you where we are going to be." Callie looks around to find Lola and spots her crouched down with the cats. "And for you, Miss Thang." Callie runs behind the tent that she and Cal are sharing and carries out a mini tent with windows made of mesh and a foam mat. "You and the cats have your own special tent that they can't run out of. Obviously, you can come and go as you please, but when you want to be with the cats, this is just for the three of you."

Cal and Jayden rush to grab the tent and mat from Callie and set it up in between the tent that Avery and James will be sharing and ours.

Callie claps again to bring everyone's focus back to her. "Happy birthday, Papa J! Hope you enjoy the show tonight!"

******

Two hours of watching Quinn and Jayden snuggle up while the guy whose voice and guitar are akin to Kenny G with his romantic and sultry sound is awful. I mean, the show that Tanya the chef put on with fire designs before, during, and after cooking our delicious meal would have been great...if I hadn't been distracted watching Jayden lean down to whisper in Quinn's ears every few minutes.

And Corbin played a great variety of songs that got everyone singing along and even dancing along to a few of them. Watching Quinn and Jayden dancing slowly to "She Will Be Loved" made me want to throw my plastic whiskey cup and hit Jayden right in the head. This did give me a little time to internally laugh at myself and realize how idiotic my thoughts are, but it didn't take long for me to end up right back in the depths of my self-pity once again.

I take a break from my own thoughts and look down to find that my drink is empty. "Be right back," I say to Reed, raising my cup in the air.

Reed nods. "Yeah, grab me another beer while you are over there."

I dip my head in acknowledgement before heading over to the bar where I find Quinn standing there looking frozen in place and Josh nowhere to be seen.

I walk over to her and place a hand on her shoulder. "You okay?" I ask.

Quinn startles and then focuses her eyes on me. Shaking the thoughts from her head, she says, "Umm. Yeah. Yeah, I am fine."

I study her face for a minute. "How have you been?"

She shrugs. "Just been keeping busy. How about you?"

I shrug as well. "Same I suppose."

Quinn makes a slow nod before looking back at the tents. She opens her mouth to say something, but I cut her off.

"Ripper?"

She cocks her head to the side. "What?"

I point to the tents. "Ripper? Why does he call you Ripper?"

She lets out a soft laugh. "Oh. The guy who… uh…."

"You don't have to say the word."

She nods. "Anyway, apparently, I got a good scratch in at some point. The nurse said there was enough of a chunk of skin under one of my nails that I definitely left a scar behind on the guy. Anyway. Um. So, Jayden calls me Ripper for Jack the Ripper." Quinn rolls her eyes and lets out another soft laugh. "Morbid I know. It was a joke that just stuck for him."

"He calls you a murderer? How romantic," I scoff.

Quinn narrows her eyes at me. "You don't get to criticize the nickname he had the chance to give me after you ghosting me left me in the situation that brought on the nickname."

Instead of that statement landing like a low blow, it turned me into a volcano, ready to erupt.

Josh chooses this moment to come back to the bar with a full bottle of Makers Mark in his hand, pours some into a cup for Quinn, and hands it to her.

Quinn raises the cup in the air. "Have the night you deserve."

With that, I lose it. Every emotion I have held in tonight explodes. Hell, every emotion I have held in for months explodes out of me.

"No, Quinn! You have the night *you* deserve!" I yell. All eyes turn to us. "I have tried and tried to talk to you. To apologize to you. To tell you what happened that night, but you never give me the chance."

I see Reed calmly walk over to Lola and pick her and the cats up before leaving the tents out of the corner of my eye.

"You do not get to keep throwing that night in my face and expecting me to keep taking each verbal blow when you have never once allowed me to tell you how fucking sorry I am."

James, Jayden, and Cal all start making their way toward us. Callie and Avery, a few steps behind them.

"I begged to be there for you. When I found out what happened…I begged to be at that hospital! To run to your side! To tell you a million times how fucking sorry I am for being an idiot and passing out from drinking too much at Ron's! I begged to come and see you when you were at your dad's house! I begged to be the one you turned to for comfort! You said no, so I honored your wishes, but I will not continue to sit here dying inside and chastising myself every God damned day if you are unwilling to give me the opportunity to even properly apologize to you!"

Avery and James are now on either side of me, pulling me back. Quinn is just blinking at me while Jayden tries to turn her to face him. Callie and Cal are moving between all of us just in case anyone decides to lunge.

James clears his throat. "Kiddo, why don't we call it a night. Jayden, will you let me know when you get her home safely?"

Jayden glares at me and then moves his gaze to James. "Yeah, of course."

Callie goes to Quinn's other side and loops her arm around Quinn's, gripping her hand tightly enough that Quinn breaks her blinking contact with me and looks over at her. "Come on babe, let's go have a girl's night. Shall we?"

Quinn slowly nods.

"Cal, will you handle all of this?" Callie asks, waving her hand around.

Cal nods. "Yeah, Jayden, could you stay with me instead and help me here? Callie can get Quinn home. Callie wasn't drinking tonight."

"That's a better plan," James chimes in. "Dove, let's walk Brad home."

Avery nods and waves at the girls. "I'll meet up with you two in a bit," she says to Quinn and Callie.

I turn and start stomping my way down the beach. After nearly a mile, I drop down into the sand and scream. Avery and James plop down beside me.

"I am disappointed with you, Brad," James says, eyes scanning the starry sky.

I can only nod because I know that he is right.

"Dove, why don't you go on and head over to be with the girls. Brad and I need to have a chat."

Avery stands and walks behind where James is sitting, bends down, kisses him on the head, and says, "Please don't do anything you will regret."

James grabs her hand, pulls it in front of his face, and kisses her wrist. "Go, Dove."

Avery pats me on the back before she heads back toward where the party was.

"I knew about the two of you. Neither of you would come out and be honest with me, so I was waiting for either of you to finally be truthful with me." James shakes his head. "I don't know why neither of you thought you could be."

"You told me you would rather take a bullet than to have me as a son-in-law," I interject.

James laughs. "That's because you called me Pops." James rubs his stomach. "You told me not to speak that into the universe after I said it, too. I can't tell if you jinxed me or if I did."

I look at his hand moving across his torso, remembering the way he looked in the hospital. "It was my fault. All of it."

James shakes his head. "I was joking."

I look up at the stars. "I'm not. It was my fault. Reed meeting Gina. Reed meeting Sandy. Bringing Gina into both of your lives. Fuck. Bringing Lola into this world where she had to witness all of this. Telling Quinn that I would meet her at the bar where she ended up getting assaulted because I drank too much and passed out like a fucking asshole. It is all my fault."

"You are an idiot if you think any of that is true. I mean you are an asshole for standing up my daughter. That part is true. But the rest of it? No. Do you really think that Gina wouldn't have sought out Reed regardless? You know how money driven that bitch was. Reed was the only single wealthy man on this island who didn't qualify for an AARP card. She would have found him no matter what. It is Gina's fault," he says pointing at his torso. "That day changed us all, but she is the only one to blame for everything that happened that day! And as for what happened to Jack…the piece of shit who assaulted her is to blame. Not you."

"If I didn't get drunk and pass out that night, I would have been there, and she would have been safe," I say softly.

"Possibly. Or you could have met up with her and both of you could have been drugged. Or there could have been someone else who was assaulted while the two of you sat inside, no wiser to what was happening to the girl outside than anyone was to what happened to Jack. We don't know what could have happened. We only know what did happen and how we can move forward from there."

"You sound like such a dad right now," I say, hoping to lighten the mood a little.

"I'll give it to you straight. I was not happy when I found out about the two of you seeing each other. Or should I say 'heard' the two of you together…." James glares at me. "But, when I calmed down and actually looked back on the few weeks leading up to that night at the lifeguard stand, I saw a sliver of my daughter again. The happy, easy going, unapologetically her side of my Jack again. I haven't seen that since she left for college."

James shifts around on the sand, eyes watching the stars, but his mind is lost in memories from the past. "I don't know the full story of what happened Jack's first month of college, but someone or something changed her. I have debated asking her a million times but always stop myself because if she wanted me to know, she would tell me. One of the downfalls of being the only parent in her life is that I have to be careful to never push anything too far. I am her *only* safe place. Even if she won't admit it, I could see that you made it into the 'safe place' category too. You may not be there now, but you can get back there."

I shrug. "I don't think she will ever let me back in long enough to try."

James leans forward, his elbows on his knees. "I know my Jack. She will at some point, but neither of us can force her into it. If you ever do get the chance to be that safe place again, don't waste it this time around. Next time, I won't try to see both sides of the story. If my daughter wasn't so stubborn, and if I didn't know your character, I wouldn't be sitting here with you right now. But I know that the last seven months have been hard for you and that you were almost back to your old self. I suggest handling your baggage before approaching Jack again."

I nod and stand. "Thank you for the talk and I am sorry I ruined your birthday…."

James cuts me off, "Ruined my birthday? Do you really think that this is where I wanted to be tonight? I would much rather have been home in my sweats or naked with my girlfriend than sitting around a fire pit watching you and Jack sneak sad glances across the flames. God, that was torturous."

I can't stop myself from chuckling. "Okay then, sorry I ruined your birthday before ruining it a different way."

James stands and claps a hand on my shoulder. "I will never admit this in front of my daughter, but I am glad you spoke your mind tonight."

I kick at the sand in front of me. "Thank you. I am glad that you don't hate me, or want to kill me, over being with your daughter and well, everything that happened."

James starts to walk away from me. "Never said I don't want to kill you for being with my daughter. Remember, I am the only parent, I have to be careful. Go get some rest, Brad."

I stand there for a minute, watching James head back to where our vehicles are before deciding to make my way back, too, just in case he changes his mind on the walk over there.

Chapter 23
Quinn

I don't know what has gotten into Jayden tonight but ever since we made it to the party, he has been overly affectionate. I can only assume it is because Brad is here. Jayden has tried to get me to dance to nearly every song Corbin has played that had any hint of romance to it. He keeps whispering the stupidest jokes in my ear that I am laughing along with just to avoid an awkward conversation right now. He even went so far as trying to feed me some of the food from his bowl. We are not "sharey" people-or at least, I'm not. It is taking everything in me not to call him out on his behavior, but I don't want to cause a scene after all the effort Callie put into making tonight perfect for all of us.

I am really sad that Chris couldn't make it, but her girlfriend being sick and wanting to take care of her definitely takes priority. It also made it to where I didn't have to share a lounge with Brad and Jayden at the same time. That would have been worse than the situation I am finding myself in now, but Brad would not have been able to sit there with Chris and her girlfriend without making some stupid sex puns. I can't help but smile thinking about Brad's stupid puns and jokes.

Jayden brushes some hair off of my cheek. "You are so beautiful when you smile like that."

My smile drops and I feel guilty. Here he is admiring me, and I am smiling about someone else. Someone who I should not even be thinking about.

I clear my throat. "I am going to go and grab another drink. I will be right back."

Jayden sits up. "Want me to go with you?"

I glance up and see that Brad is watching Corbin. "No, don't want people to think we are sneaking off for nefarious reasons."

Jayden looks over towards Brad and Reed. "Would that be so bad?"

I study Jayden's face for a second. "Is that why you have been putting on this little show tonight?"

Jayden shakes his head, but I don't give him a chance to answer before I slide off the lounge and walk toward the bar.

"Josh, can I get another Makers?"

Josh grabs the bottle, realizing it is empty, he puts a finger in the air and says, "Don't move," before dashing towards a truck.

I don't know what it was about him saying those two words that triggered me to shut down, but it was like I could feel my body just…stop. Like my brain needed to pause all bodily functions so that it could process something that I didn't know it needed to process.

"You okay?"

I am startled out of my mental reboot. "Umm. Yeah. Yeah, I am fine."

Brad stares at me for a while before asking, "How have you been?"

I shrug. "Just been keeping busy. How about you?"

He mimics my shrug. "Same I suppose."

I nod and look back to where the tents are, hoping no one is watching us, but also kind of hoping someone will come over to break up this awkward encounter. Since no one is coming to save me, I get ready to excuse myself when Brad cuts me off.

"Ripper?"

"What?"

He points to where everyone is sitting. "Ripper? Why does he call you Ripper?"

I can't help but laugh at the origin of the nickname. "Oh. The guy who…uh…." How do I say "the guy who assaulted me when you stood me up" to Brad?

Brad makes it a little easier on me. "You don't have to say the word."

"Anyway, apparently, I got a good scratch in at some point. The nurse said there was enough of a chunk of skin under one of my nails that I definitely left a scar behind on the guy. Anyway. Um. So, Jayden calls me Ripper for Jack the Ripper."

I can't help but roll my eyes and giggle a little at the memory of Jayden calling me Jack the Ripper as a term of badassery when he overheard the nurse tell me about the skin under my fingernail. Jayden popped his head in the barely cracked door with a fist pump and whisper yelled, "Jack the Ripper over here! Get it girl!"

I focus my attention back on Brad. "Morbid I know. It was a joke that just stuck for him. "

Brad sneers, "He calls you a murderer? How romantic."

Is this guy fucking serious right now? "You don't get to criticize the nickname he had the chance to give me after you ghosting me left me in the situation that brought on the nickname."

If I had a drink in my hand, I would throw it on him right now. Luckily for Brad, the time it takes for Josh to make it back to the bar, pour my drink, and hand it to me gave me just enough time to realize he isn't worth wasting alcohol over.

I raise my cup in the air and say the first sentence that ever ruffled Brad. "Have the night you deserve."

I watch Brad's face for a second, hoping to catch a glance of that raw pain that I wanted to inflict on him, something to give me the satisfaction that I have hurt him even the tiniest bit. I wasn't prepared, though, for his anger.

"No, Quinn! You have the night *you* deserve!" He screams at me. "I have tried and tried to talk to you. To apologize to you. To tell you what happened that night, but you never give me the chance. You do not get to keep throwing that night in my face and expecting me to keep taking each verbal blow when you have never once allowed me to tell you how fucking sorry I am. I begged to be there for you. When I found out what happened…I begged to be at that hospital! To run to your side! To tell you a million times how fucking sorry I am for being an idiot and passing out from drinking too much at Ron's! I begged to come and see you when you were at your dad's house! I begged to be the one you turned to for comfort! You said no so I honored your wishes, but I will not continue to sit here dying inside and chastising myself every God damned day if

"Why?" I ask, crawling to my knees so I can see over the back of my couch and into the kitchen. "What happened?"

Avery rummages around in my fridge for the juice to add to her rum. "Testosterone overload. I am really hoping your dad doesn't hurt Brad too badly." Avery stands and shrugs. "I mean a little badly would be okay, just not too badly."

"Hey, Avery? Can I ask you something and you promise to tell me the whole truth?" I ask.

Avery whips around. "Have I ever been anything less than completely transparent with you?"

I contemplate her question for a split second and shake my head knowing she truly never has.

Avery leans a hip against my kitchen counter, leaving her drink mixing abandoned, giving me her full attention. "Ask away then, hun."

I run a hand through my hair. "Tonight, Brad claimed that he tried to come see me at the hospital. Do you know anything about that?"

Avery doesn't even blink. "Of course. I told him not to. Your dad was one wrong heartbeat away from a full-on heart attack that day. I didn't want Brad coming in proving that he was the one who had stood you up." Avery tilts her head to the side in silent contemplation. "Although, had I known then what I know now, I may have told Brad to come."

I gasp out, "What, so Dad could pummel him?"

Avery shakes her head with wide eyes. "No, I didn't know then that your dad knew about the two of you."

I choke on my own spit. "What? What do you mean dad knew about us?"

Avery turns back to her ingredients and starts mixing her drink together. "Babe! Your dad figured out that you two had a thing going a long time ago but didn't tell me until you were staying at our house."

"How did he find out?" I yelp.

Avery stares at me like it's obvious for a second then dramatically stirs her drink to give me a moment to figure it out on my own. When I don't, I ask her again.

"How did he find out?"

Avery dramatically huffs out a breath and then looks at me like I'm an idiot. "Who do you think told Brad where to find the painting?"

I shrug. "Dad?"

Avery nods slowly, still waiting for it to click. "And why would your dad point Brad in the direction of someone who had a jellyfish painting?"

I shake my head but answer, "He heard Brad call me Jellyfish?"

Avery makes a twirling motion with her hands signaling for me to stay on that line of thinking. "And the other nickname."

"Jelly?" I ask, raising an eyebrow, wondering why Jelly would give away our relationship…I feel the blood drain from my face. "Oh my God! He heard us in the shack! Brad called me Jelly when we were having sex."

Callie laughs, reminding me that she was even here. Avery waves a finger in the air. "Ding ding ding!"

I can't decide if I want to puke or cry. "Someone go dig a hole for me to jump into. Please."

Callie fully joins the conversation now. "Why do you keep asking about Brad and the hospital?"

I look between Callie and Avery before admitting to them why. "I thought he never even cared." I start drawing patterns on the couch cushion to help keep my emotions in check. Like my little couch doodles are holding back the tears as long as my fingers keep moving, occupying the part of my brain that controls bodily functions or something. "I always refused to see him at your house because I thought he never tried to see me…when I was at the hospital, I mean. I figured he would realize something was up when I didn't come home. He never called me back. I just assumed that he didn't care at first…and then when I knew he knew, I figured he was trying to feel less guilty for not putting in effort to see me." I shake my head. "Honestly, I don't know what all I was, or even am, feeling about this."

Avery walks over to me, placing her hand on mine, effectively stopping my couch doodling. "Brad begged me for information. I am so sorry that I never told you or properly relayed that to you. I truly believed that I was doing the right thing at the hospital by telling him not to come, and when you were staying at our house, I only asked if you wanted me to get your dad out so that you could decide if you wanted to see him without any pressure from knowing that Brad was desperate to talk to you. I thought that if you knew the extent of his desperation, that you would feel obligated to hear him out, even if you didn't want to, and I didn't want to make you feel that way. I am so extremely sorry about that. I truly only did it with the best of intentions."

I lean up and wrap my arms around what I can reach of Avery. I don't know if it is to reassure her or myself. "I know that. I do."

I hear Avery sniffle and glance up to see her wiping away a tear.

"Don't cry," I whisper.

Avery shakes her head. "I can't help it. I feel so foolish. I sat there watching both of you hurt so deeply and I was part of the cause of it."

I stand from the couch and make my way to Avery, wrapping my arms around her and squeezing her tightly to me, forcing her to *feel* the conviction behind my words. "You never caused any of my pain. The pain Brad and I bear is from our own doing, and from the piece of shit rapist out there. Not you."

Avery squeezes me back, just as tightly.

Callie blows her nose behind us. "Fuck both of you bitches right now! I just started my period today and am too hormonal for all of this," she says, waving her tissue in our direction.

Avery and I both laugh and open our arms closest to Callie, inviting her into our hug circle. Callie blows her nose one more time before joining us.

"Alright, heifers. If we are going to be sappy sobbers tonight, we need to at least be prepared." Avery points to Callie. "Queue up Beaches and grab the tissues." Avery points at me. "Go grab throw blankets, face masks, and spare pillows." Avery turns her hand to point at herself.

"I will make some drinks and popcorn." Then in true Avery fashion, she smacks her own ass.

Callie and I smack our own asses for shits and giggles before doing what Avery said to do.

******

"Woah, what happened in here?" I hear Dad say from somewhere in my house.

I blink open an eye to find that me and the girls are all sprawled out across my couches and floor. Avery still has a face mask on; popcorn is all over the floor along with some candy wrappers, and what looks to be some sort of jelly covered Nutter Butter…I think.

A pillow flies by my head and hits Jayden, who apparently invited himself to come over with my dad.

"Oooops. Sorry, that was meant for the squawking dinosaur over there," Avery laughs out, hand drifting to her face where I am sure the dried-out face mask is tugging.

"Dove, you will pay for the old jokes," Dad says.

Avery smiles and winks.

I don't know if it's the fact that I am listening to my dad and his girlfriend, whom I have come to consider one of my best friends, flirting that is making me need to puke or if it is all the rum we drank last night during Beaches and Steel Magnolias. Fried Green Tomatoes was our next pick for "who needs a man" movie night, but we never made it that far before apparently passing out.

Jayden makes his way to me but before he can touch me, I jump off the couch. The puke won't wait.

Callie hops up behind me. "I will call Cal to bring the hydration station."

******

Later that night, after I am hydrated thanks to Cal's secret medical supply hook-up, I am laying under Jayden while he fucks me, but my mind is on Brad. Fucking would be generous. It is more like he is unrhythmically pumping into me while I lay here bored out of my mind. Hence, my mind drifting to Brad. Remembering his hand gripping my jaw after he stuffed my own panties in my mouth. Picturing the appreciation on his face every time he watched me cum. Remembering the push and pull of who holds the power every time we made love…made love.

My mind wanders off to the last time Brad and I were together, when I *needed* him and that is exactly what we did. We made love to each other.

That realization brings me back to the present. To the man who is breaking a sweat over the most lackluster sex, yet again, of my life. I pat his shoulder to get his attention off of my boobs and on my face.

"I want to break up," I state flatly.

Jayden stops his mediocre pump and stares at me for a second. "Are you serious? Because I really can't tell right now."

I nod. "Serious."

Jayden glances down. "I am still inside of you, and you decide that this is the time to mention this?"

I nod again. "Yep."

Jayden instantly goes limp and pulls out of me. Running a hand through his hair for a second before pulling the condom off of him. "Do I get to know what happened, while we were fucking, that brought this on?"

I sit up, without covering myself, and shrug. "I am just not feeling this. I truly don't think I ever was, but you felt safe. Like a safe choice. I think it is some weird crush I developed because I thought you were good for me after everything that happened."

Jayden scoffs and stands from my bed. "So, you didn't ever actually like me, it was just because I was the one who found you?"

I reach out to put a hand on his arm, but he jerks back from me. "Not completely and definitely not on purpose. I think that with everything that happened, and the fact that we had already started building a friendship foundation, it all just…I don't know…compounded into an attachment that I thought was romantic feelings but was more just…gratitude."

Jayden drops his head for a second before meeting my eyes again and nods. "For what it's worth, I had a lot of fun with you."

I move to grab a robe. I feel like what I say next needs to be a clothed statement. "I did too, and I hope that we can remain friends. I truly do enjoy your company, just not in the way I pushed us into."

Jayden slides his pants on. "Yeah, I think we can manage that."

Once he is clothed, I walk over to give him a hug. I meant what I said, I truly do enjoy his company, and when it is the whole group, he kind of completes us. He was a missing piece to our friendship to balance us all out.

"For what it's worth, I am glad that we at least tried this route. Better that we know now and all of that," Jayden says into my hair.

I nod against his chest. "Agree."

Chapter 24
Brad

I look over to see my door shaking from the force of whoever is pounding on it from the other side. Shifting my gaze up a little, I see an empty bottle of Jack Daniels sitting on my nightstand. *When did I buy a bottle of Jack?* My focus is pulled back to the door when I hear Avery's murmuring on the other side instead of the constant pounding.

"Don't want to open the damned door? I will show you. I watched enough YouTube videos that I can pick nearly any lock now, sucka. Just. One. More. There."

I watch as my door slowly swings open and Avery stays crouched in front of it for a moment, look of smug accomplishment on her face before she brings her eyes to mine. Hers change instantly. My brain is slow right now but if I had to pick an emotion, I would call that pure anger. She is pissed at me.

I attempt to roll over but can't because a body is blocking me.

Avery throws clothes at the person behind me. Looks like a dress or something. "Get the hell up and out of this house. NOW!" She screams.

I feel the bed shift behind me and some groaning. "You didn't say that you have a girlfriend."

I want to puke the second I recognize that voice.

Avery crosses her arms over her chest and sneers, "I'm not his girlfriend, I just refuse to associate with trash. So, get the hell out so I can have a little intervention with my friend here. He obviously needs one since he allowed you in his bed."

I have never seen Avery this mad, or this rude, but I actually kind of like it.

Tiffany leans over from behind me and kisses my cheek. "Call me later."

I don't say a word. If I open my mouth, I will vomit.

Avery and I watch Tiffany leave my room and I hear Reed escorting Tiffany out of the house. Avery turns back to me, bends down, grabs a pair of my dirty pants, and throws them at my face.

"Cover the hell up. We are having a chat. Meet me in the living room when you are decent." Avery turns around and leaves my room.

I sit myself up on the side of the bed for a moment to catch my bearings. *What the fuck did I do last night after leaving James's party?*

I put on the dirty pants, run into the bathroom for the longest piss of my life, and then make my way to the living room where I find Avery, Reed, and Brad.

I glance around at everyone. "You weren't joking about the intervention," I laugh out.

"I'm done with your bullshit," Avery states.

I pad towards the kitchen. "Well, let me make my morning coffee and then we can start this 'come to Jesus' chat."

I look at the clock and notice the time. It is nearly eight at night. Where did my entire day go?

I nod toward Lola's room. "She in bed already? Do we need to censor ourselves for this?"

Reed shakes his head. "She's with Chris and Candace, but I am glad to see that you finally have the wherewithal to even consider Lola. That would have helped about..." Reed looks at the clock on the wall. "Sixteen hours ago, when you and Tiffany woke her up, barging into the house, knocking over everything you passed. Or even fifteen hours ago when you woke her up again, carrying on about how you won that hand of strip poker and you were ready to see some titties. Actually, fourteen hours ago would have been even better. You could have saved her from hearing you and Tiffany fuck against the wall the connects to her bedroom." Reed snaps his fingers. "Yeah, that would have been a much better time to take Lola into consideration."

I lean over the sink and puke. The one person I swore I would never let see the worst side of me did. The one person I wanted to shield from my laundry list of bad decisions. When I have nothing left to throw up, I rinse my mouth out with tap water and then turn to face my friends. If I can even call them that anymore.

I run a hand through my hair and down my face. "I am so sorry, Reed. I can't…."

"You are always '*so sorry*', yet you never do anything to change the path, Brad. You just keep rolling down the same self-sabotaging road."

I can't do anything but nod.

"When is enough actually enough? I have picked you up from bars on so many different occasions, or watched you stumble in on others where I should have picked you up, so you weren't putting everyone around you at risk on the road. Lola and I have listened to you hurl the contents of your stomach up too many nights to count. Or how about all the times you have said you would grab something and come home, but instead spent the night at the bar, and walk out of your room the next morning empty-handed. How many times have you had to 'make it up' to Lola? In the beginning, I understood. We were all just trying to cope in any way that we could. To figure out how we would make it without Sandy," Reed pauses long enough to wave his hand in my direction, "but this…Brad; it has to stop. I can't do *this* anymore. I can't have Lola subjected to *this* anymore."

I push my hands in my pockets to hide my balled-up fists. I am not mad at Reed; I am mad at myself.

Avery punches James in the arm and then urges him to go next.

"I really thought that after our talk last night, that you would have come home and done some self-reflecting or something." James shakes his head. "I really thought that we got somewhere last night." James finally looks at me. "I didn't realize that I needed to babysit you after the conversation we had."

I turn my head to face the wall for a moment. I need to reel myself in before I cry, or worse, go on a verbal rampage.

Avery jumps to her feet, grabs the remote from the coffee table, and throws it at me. Then she turns and grabs a book from the coffee table, throwing that at me too. Followed by one of Lola's shoes, a random toy, a coaster, and finally a pillow because that is the only thing close enough to her.

I take the hit of every item silently, watching her anger rise higher and higher.

She points her rage filled finger at me but before she can get a single word out, the tears she has been holding back burst out of her. "Quit being so fucking selfish! I lost her, Brad! I can't lose you! I will not survive if I lose you, too!"

Avery falls to the ground, gripping her chest and stomach. I run to one side of her while James falls to her other side.

"I need you! Brad, I need you to fill her shoes for me. I need you to be here, to be my best friend. I need you back. I don't like this version; this isn't *MY BRAD*. I need you back. To help me hold on to the fun last memories we have of her. To cry about the sad last memories we have of her. I can't keep holding these all in by myself. I can't keep waiting for you to be ready. Please, Brad, don't make me lose you. Come back to me," Avery cries out, gripping her chest so hard she is cutting into her own skin.

Reed stands up and attempts to leave the room, but Avery's scream halts him.

"No! No! You do not get to walk out of this room! You sit your ass back down!"

Reed follows Avery's command.

Avery points to each of us in the room. "I have given all of you the strong me, the happy me, and the supportive me. None of you get to take from me without giving in return any longer."

Avery points to Reed. "You are the reason I am stuck with those sad memories being the last ones I have of her. You do not get to shy away from them now."

I push Avery's hand down to her side. "Avery, don't say that."

Avery whips her head to me and screams, "Don't say what? Don't place blame on anyone? Don't be upset that I lost my best friend?"

I jump to my feet, hitting my chest with my fists. "I am to blame for all of it! All of it! It's all my fault!" I scream out.

Everyone stills and stares at me.

"Everyone is dead, or hurting, or angry because of me. It is all because of me!"

Reed cautiously approaches me. "Brad, none of this is your fault," he says softly, his hands slowly moving to my shoulders.

I smack his hands away. "It is. I forced you into going on that date with Gina because I was selfish. Just like I forced you to go to the beach with me the day we met Sandy and Avery. All because I was bored. I found out later that day that Sandy was your new nanny, and I didn't tell you because I wanted to see what happened." I run both of my hands through my hair. "I was so goddamn bored that I didn't tell you because I thought that watching you two find out would give me entertainment."

I start pacing the living room. "I told you so many times that I had a bad feeling about Gina, but I never pushed you when you didn't want to hear it. I didn't want to be the downer friend, so I just sat back and kept watching it all happen." I stop and face everyone, throwing my arms out wide and scream, "And look what happened! Look what fucking happened! Sandy is dead because of it. I hurt all of you!"

I point to James. "You nearly died because of me! I nearly left the one woman I have ever loved an orphan because of it!"

I point to Reed. "And you! If the cops hadn't busted in when they did, forcing Gina to react and choose to shoot herself, who knows what would have happened to you! Where would that have left Lola?!"

I point to Avery and fall to my knees in front of her. "And you," I whisper, "I cost you the one person in this world who was worthy of your love and friendship. I promised you the night that she came home from jail that I would always watch out for her, for you both, and I have let you down." I wipe away the tears falling down my own face now. "I am so sorry for lying to you."

Avery stares at me, dumbfounded for a minute before reaching out and smacking me across the face. I am too stunned to move so I just take a moment, my head still facing away from her from the power behind that slap. Slowly, I turn my head to face her, and James moves to kneel in front of her, to protect her from me.

I pull a hand up to my cheek where the lingering burn is. "Did you just slap me?"

Avery tries to hide a giggle behind the hand she brought to her lips. "I don't know why I did that, but it felt needed."

I rub at the sting. "What? Why?"

"To smack some damn sense into you, obviously," she states matter of factly.

Reed joins in on her laughing, followed by James. I am staring at the three people in this room with me and wondering how it went from an intervention about my drinking to me being the only sane person in here.

James is the first to break his laughing off, cocking his head to the side, staring at me intently. "Did you just say you love my daughter?"

The whole room falls silent.

I nod.

Reed moves to put himself between me and James. "I think we should all take a moment…." Reed starts.

"Did you ever tell her?" James asks, catching everyone by surprise.

I shake my head.

Avery reaches out and smacks me again.

I grab my other cheek. "Can we be done with the physical violence yet?"

Avery points a finger in my face. "No, you actually deserved that one. You should have told her."

I throw my hands out in the air. "When did I have the chance?"

Avery puts her hands over James' ears, like he can't hear her regardless. "The night in the shack."

James shakes his head.

Reed's eyes are bouncing between everyone so much, I am afraid they may bounce right out of his head. "Wait. Everyone knew?"

I point to Reed. "You knew, too?"

Reed scoffs. "How could I not? These walls are pretty damn thin."

James makes a gagging noise.

I defeatedly raise my hands in the air. "Well, now that we all got everything out of our systems, does anyone have anything they want to add? Because I would really like it if this is the last time something like this happens," I say, waving around the room.

Reed clears his throat. "Lola and I are moving out tomorrow."

I reach a hand towards Reed. "Dude, you don't have to do that. I am so sorry, and I will apologize to Lola. I swear it will never happen again."

Reed shakes his head. “Not because of that. Our house is done. The furniture was delivered and put together today.”

I chew on my bottom lip for a second before responding, “Oh, well…the house won’t be the same without you guys. This place will be so...quiet."

Reed scoffs. "It is always quiet until you walk in the room."

James laughs out, "Isn’t that the truth?!"

Avery smacks his arm.

James pulls his arm in to cradle it. “I thought we were done with the physical violence?”

Avery crosses her arms over her chest. “I never said I was; besides, it is making me feel wayyyyy better. Maybe I need to find an outlet along these lines.”

I turn to face James and Avery. “Do you two have anything else to air out? Hidden pregnancy? Upcoming wedding?”

Avery’s nose scrunches in disgust. “Kids? Ewwww. I’m not made to be a mom to humans. I can’t answer the other one because I have no intention of being the one to propose, so that’s up to him,” she says, pointing towards James. “But I do need to apologize to you, Brad.”

I cock my head to the side. "What could you possibly need to apologize for? Pretty sure that I am the one who has screwed up lately."

Avery fidgets with her fingers. "When I told you not to come to the hospital, I did not have the right to do that. I thought I was doing the right thing, but I think I made things worse for you and Jackie."

I walk over to Avery and dip down so I can be eye level with her. "Why would you ever think that, Davey?"

Avery raises her chin before whispering out, "Because part of the reason she refused to hear you out is because she thought that you didn't try to see her at the hospital. She thought you didn't care at first. And that is my fault."

I wrap my arms around Avery and squeeze her tightly to me. "It is not your fault! Do you hear me? When it comes to how I handled what happened between me and Quinn, that is all on me. I could have ignored you. I should have ignored you and broken through every door to get to Quinn."

Avery shrugs. "I think that you and her need to have a conversation about things. I think she is ready."

I glance over at James, and he nods, agreeing with Avery.

Chapter 25
Quinn

After escorting Jayden out of my house, I ran to the shower, wanting to wash him off of me as fast as possible. One thing that tonight forced me to realize is that I love Brad. I don't want to continue this avoidance or animosity loop that we have found ourselves in. I want us to work things out. No. I need us to work things out.

After I feel thoroughly cleaned, I slip into a maxi dress, slide into a pair of sandals, and begin to walk towards Brad's house. The walk will take me about twenty minutes, but I need this time to figure out what I want to say to him. How I want to say it. Even though I know I want him back in my life, I need to figure out at what capacity.

I have my speech planned and rehearsed by the time I turn on the street that Brad, Avery, and Dad live on. I am just in front of Avery and Dad's when I see a woman leaving Brad's front door. Not just any woman. Fucking Tiffany.

I turn around and start my walk back to my house. I am too late. I can't even blame him. I made him sit there and watch Jayden and me. The one man he already hated so much. And I practically paraded Jayden in front of him.

This is the karma I deserve.

Chapter 26
Brad
One Month Later

I walk into my classroom for the first time in months. We have a week before school starts, and I am ready to get this new school year started. I carry my totes of decorations to my classroom before I decide to head over to the lounge to get another cup of coffee. I need all the energy I can get for today. I decided that this new version of me, and the new school year, deserves a classroom revamp.

My classroom has looked the same the entirety of my time teaching here. It is overdue for a new look. Between the meetings and professional development courses throughout this week, my free time will be spent changing my room around to bring some new life to it.

I am hitting the "brew" button on a fresh pot of coffee when I hear the squeal of Barbara from the doorway.

"Oh, my Brad! Look at you! This summer did you well, my dear!" Barbara says as she runs over and wraps her arms around me. "You look like you again!"

I throw an arm around the old woman. "Don't butter me up too much, Barb. It will make my head big."

Barbara reaches up and pinches my cheeks with tears in her big, brown eyes. "Oh, I have missed you so much!"

I hug her back into me. "Don't get sappy. We can't let everyone else know that I am your favorite."

Barbara lets out a soft laugh and before composing herself. "Actually, Callie was my favorite."

I pull my hand to my chest in mock shock. "How dare you? Wait…was?"

Barbara nods. "Yeah, I am going to miss having her around."

I shake my head. "Barbara, she is coming back this year."

Barbara looks at me like I have two heads. "No, she isn't, dear. I mean, she was, but apparently, she changed her mind last week."

"Then who will our nurse be?" I ask.

Barbara shrugs her curled shoulders. "No idea, they didn't say anything to me except that she won't be here til next week."

******

When I decorated my classroom to feel like the kids were sitting around a campfire singing, to include pillows that look like tree stumps, I never took into consideration that the younger kids might decide to use the old harmonica boxes I painted to look like bricks as projectiles. It wouldn't have been so bad had the little kids also not decided to put things inside the empty boxes…which led me to my first visit to the nurse's office on the first day of school.

I walk in holding a paper towel to the cut right above my eyebrow that is bleeding and find the mysterious new nurse. She is an older woman, short and rotund.

She points to the chair next to the nurse's table. "Take a seat hun, the nurse will be right back."

I sit where she pointed to. "You aren't the nurse?"

The woman shakes her head. "No, I'm the new director over the cafeteria. The nurse went to grab some paper so I can have an updated copy of the known allergies. I like to have paper copies too, in case we lose power or there's a glitch in the system. Can't trust these computers you know."

I nod. "Loud and clear. Completely agree."

The rotund woman glances behind me. "Ah, there she is."

I turn around to see my Quinnie walking into the nurse's office. When her eyes find mine, they go from relief to concern within seconds.

"What happened to you?" Quinn asks as she rushes over to me.

"It looks worse than it is, I promise," I say.

Quinn grabs some gloves, quickly sliding them on. "Judging by the amount of blood seeping through that paper towel, I might disagree."

"My vision is fine, no pain, I don't feel dizzy…it really just looks bad."

Quinn removes the paper towel and cringes. "What happened?"

"One of my second graders filled one of my firepit boxes with rocks, and then one of my kinder kids decided to *let it go* during 'Let It Go.'"

Quinn lets out a soft laugh.

"You got your hands full here, hun. Mind if I swing by in the morning to grab these? I need to run over to the middle school too," the woman I forgot was even here says behind Quinn.

Quinn glances over her shoulder. "Yeah, Tanya, I will have them all ready for you by then. I am so sorry about the delay."

Tanya tsks. "No worry, hun. I kind of sprung this on you. See you tomorrow."

Quinn dips her head toward Tanya before bringing her attention back to my head. "You could probably use some stitches to be completely honest."

I pull my head back from her hands. "Seriously?"

Quinn gives a single shrug of her shoulders. "Yeah. You can get by with some glue if we can get this bleeding to stop, but if we can't, stitches will be needed."

I huff out, "You gotta be shittin' me."

Quinn's eyes go wide, and she slaps her hand over my mouth. "Brad!"

I wince. "Sorry," I mumble from behind her hand.

"I think the bleeding has clotted enough here. Want me to glue it or do you want to try the butterfly bandages?"

I give her a cocky grin. "You are the professional, you tell me."

One side of her lip gives away the smile she is fighting. "Glue it is. Don't move."

I sit there silently while she glues up the cut and wait for her to step back, admire her work, and head to the sink before asking her what I have been holding in for too long. "So, could I take you to dinner…or for a coffee…anywhere really so we can talk?"

Quinn falters and huffs out a laugh. "I don't know if that is necessary."

"And why is that?"

Quinn shakes her head and glances at the door before bringing her attention back to me. She opens her mouth to speak when a little boy holding his stomach walks in and then barfs all over the floor.

Quinn runs a hand across her brow. "Well then, kiddo, I think I know what brings you in," she says, walking over and picking up the little boy.

Quinn puts him on the table before turning her attention back to me. "See ya around," she says to me in dismissal.

Chapter 27
Quinn

When Callie told me she had my Halloween costume handled after her, Cal, and Jayden decided on our theme without me, I should have known to question everything and agree to nothing. Had I followed that sentiment, I wouldn't be standing here in a white bodysuit onesie that has 23 in blood red across the chest with a white tutu that looks like it belongs on a child. Oh, and let's not forget the Happy Birthday cone hat.

Growing up, I was always able to skip my birthday with my peers since they were always distracted with my birthday falling on Halloween. Only my dad, Callie, Cal, and their parents even told me Happy Birthday, and I was content with that.

After going a little over the top with my red lips, and adding falsies to my lashes, I do a last look in the mirror. My hair is curled under the birthday hat, I added the body shimmer that Callie insisted I wear, my ass is barely covered in the bodysuit and micro tutu, but it does look good. I dig around in my closet to find the finishing touch to the outfit: my red chunky platform heels that I used to wear when

Callie and I would dress up and pretend to be Spice Girls. I look like a sexy birthday nurse.

I walk out into the living room, excited to see what everyone else is wearing. Callie is in a red mini bodycon dress, her red chunky heels that match my own, with a headband that looks like a flame on top.

She throws her arms out wide and spins for me. "What do you think? I'm a birthday candle!"

"You look hot," I say with a giggle.

Callie swats at the air in mock modesty. "You're so punny."

Cal laughs, drawing my attention to him. He is dressed in a shiny silver suit.

"And you are?" I ask him.

Cal reaches in his pocket and throws a handful of confetti over my head. "I'm a confetti cannon. Obviously."

I point to my living room floor. "You are cleaning that up."

"I am shedding everywhere. I'm going to be naked by the end of the night, Callie," Jayden says, walking into the living room, leaving a trail of tissue paper behind him.

"You won't be naked, you are wearing a nude-colored bodysuit," Callie retorts.

Jayden huffs. "That is plastered to my body and looks like I am naked…."

I shrug. "At least you have a good body."

Callie snorts. "Don't objectify my boyfriend."

It is still weird to me that Callie and Jayden decided to start dating last month. When they approached me to talk, I was worried that they were going to go into some intervention about my moping around but instead asked my permission to date. Like I had any say in that. If I were truly honest with myself, I knew that they were better suited to begin with, but I wasn't in the right frame of mind five months ago to register that.

"I will take Ripper's objectifying over Gertie's! You know she gets touchy after two cosmos. Last time she pinched my ass, I had a bruise for nearly three weeks," Jayden exclaims.

"I can't wait to hear her explain all the ways she wants to bust the piñata to get to the goodies inside tonight," Cal laughs out, pointing a finger towards the crotch of Jayden's piñata costume.

Jayden's eyes go wide. "Trade me costumes," he frantically pleads to Cal.

Cal shakes his head.

Jayden turns to Callie. "Babe, come on. I'll wear the dress, switch me. I can't have Gertie trying to get my goodies."

Callie throws her head back and laughs. "Sorry, *Babe.* I will just burn her if she gets too close," Callie jokes, walking over to Jayden and patting his crotch.

Cal and I both make a gagging sound.

"Well," I say, "of all the themes you guys could have chosen, this is the lamest…but I do think we all look pretty fucking dapper."

Callie makes a roping motion in the air. "Alright. Uber is here. To the Roost!"

On the walk out the front door Cal leans in to ask me, "Are you sure you are okay with the venue?"

I nod. "I have been back a few times. I won't let what happened there rule my life in any way."

Cal throws an arm around my shoulder and tugs me in for a hug. "I am so proud of you. I hope I can be as strong as you when I grow up."

I smack his chest and growl. "We are the same age; you are just as grown as I am."

Cal shakes his head. "No way, you are way more grown up than I am. I just hide my Peter Pan Syndrome behind the white coat, so I seem more grown up."

******

The Roost is packed when we arrive, and I can feel a tiny bit of anxiety creeping up on me. Callie walks in past me, grabbing my hand, and dragging me behind her.

"Our table is just over there," she yells, pointing towards the table that has balloons floating above it and tied to the chairs, resembling the house from Up.

"I never would have guessed which one was ours," I yell over the roar of the crowd.

Callie whips her head around to stick her tongue out at me.

I scan the bar and spot Patsy standing behind the bar, waving us to come over to see her. I squeeze Callie's hand and point towards Patsy.

"Look at all of you! My babies!" Patsy coos over us.

"Hey Gran," Callie and Cal say in their creepy twin unison way.

Patsy swats at the air. "Keep your voices down, I can't let people know I am old enough to have grown grandchildren. What does everyone want? First round is on me."

We give Patsy our orders, take a round of shots at the bar, then grab our beers, and head to our table.

The singers have been fun tonight. Most are staying in theme of their costumes. There are a ton of Swifties in here tonight. Seems a group of girls are celebrating every era. The Village People group looks fabulous. The old school mobsters are belting out some Frankie Valli and Sinatra. Of course, Ron is demanding everyone's attention. He is dressed in a black suit, a black witch's hat, and has green eye shadow, blush, and lipstick on, belting "Defying Gravity" with all green lighting on him. He is a wonderful sight to see, voice to hear, and weight to feel on my chest.

Like my thoughts of him conjured him, Brad walks into the bar. After a scan of the area closest to the door, he makes his way to the bar where he talks to Patsy for a few minutes before walking towards the table next to the front door, drink in hand.

Even though I try to hide my eyes, and mind, from wandering back over to where he is, Callie not only notices, but decides it needs to be brought to the table's attention."

"Quit being Quinn and be Jackie-O."

I look at her quizzically. "What do you mean?"

Callie nods her head in Brad's direction. "Quit being Quinn, the girl who was forced to be demure on the outside. Bring back Jackie-O, the girl who doesn't give a damn about what people think."

I take a drink of my beer and contemplate what Callie just said. She is the only one who knows why "Quinn" came to be. Well, who Quinn came to be is more like it. I chose to use that nickname when I started college, I felt Jack and Jackie were juvenile sounding names. Unfortunately, the first, and only, guy I actually dated felt I was too juvenile for him. Everything I did, he would have a problem with. "You need to dress like an adult, quit living in band tees." "Can you tone down your need for sex? It is not normal." "Why can't you quit the bar? The library job is more respectable." "You need to sell the Harley and get a car. You aren't a heathen."

After a year of him criticizing every single thing about me, I became a shell of myself. When I was finally able to recognize it, I hated myself for it. I swore then that I would never let anyone change me and began the journey of finding myself again. I thought that I had, but judging by what Callie just said, I still am not there yet.

I take one more sip and nod. "You are right. I'll be back," I say as Cal finishes singing "Firework" by Katy Perry, complete with confetti flying every time he sings the word "firework."

I am halfway through the crowd, making my way to Brad when someone bumps into me. Thanks to the chunky heels, rather than just falling, I get a couple of wobbly steps in while trying to catch myself. Unfortunately, my POTS kicks in when I make it from my crouched position back to standing, and I drop into someone's arms. Fortunately, I don't faint though.

"Whoa, Jackie. You okay?" Josh asks, arms around my waist.

"Yeah," I say, grabbing his hands to release me when I feel a scar. I whip my head back around and look at Josh, hand roaming over that recognizable scar before I lunge my body forward, falling to the ground.

I point up at him. "You! You? Why?" I am crawling away, putting as much distance between us as I can while I stumble to get to my feet.

The crowd has parted, bringing everyone's attention to us. I see Callie, Cal, and Jayden making their way through everyone before I feel familiar arms wrap around me and pull me to my feet.

I turn my head to see Brad, and he must notice the fear on my face. He immediately turns me around, hiding me from the crowd with his body.

"What is it? What's wrong?" he asks, eyes roaming my face for a clue.

With a wobbly whisper I tell him, "It was Josh. It was Josh."

Without needing further explanation, Brad knows what I am referring to too. In a blink, he has left me, and tackled Josh to the ground. Cal runs over to Brad while Callie runs to me. Jayden stands between us to figure out what is going on.

"Call the detective you have been working with. Now! Pats! Throw me some tape! Now!" Brad roars out.

Callie looks at me, eyes full of questions. I just grab her hand and rub the spot where Josh's scar is. That is all I have to do for her to know what I am silently telling her. She glances over at Brad on top of Josh and then back at me. Tears free falling down her cheeks, her free hand pulled up to her mouth, holding in the words she wants to scream right now too.

"Take my car, get the girls home!" Patsy hollers over the crowd.

Jayden protectively pulls us over to the bar with him to grab Patsy's keys and then towards the door. The path clears before us as murmurs surround us.

"What the fuck is going on?" Harley whispers to the Joker

"Do you think he had something to do with what happened with Raven?" Lilo asks Stitch

"Whatever it was, I'm sure he deserves what he's getting, he has always been a creep." One of the Swifties proclaims.

"Brad looks like he is ready to rip him to shreds." M3GAN says.

This last whisper I hear in passing has me halting my steps.

"What are you doing?" Jayden asks me.

Callie looks at me, concern in her eyes.

"I have to see if I left a scar."

Callie tilts her head. "Left a scar?"

I nod. "Yeah, I need to know if my scratch left a scar. I need to see if he has something to remember me by."

I turn around and sprint to where Brad and Cal are holding Josh down on the ground while another patron tapes his hands together.

"Let me see where I got you!" I demand.

Josh refuses to acknowledge that I said anything to him, so I step forward, put my heel on his sternum, and give it some pressure until I see him wince.

"Let. Me. See. It."

Josh tries to wiggle out from under my heel, so I give it just a little bit more weight.

"On my arm. Inside of my left arm," he whines out.

I give a good thump of my heel to his chest before I crouch down and pull his sleeve up to see the jagged little scar. It's no bigger than a quarter but I smile.

I bend down so my lips are mere millimeters from his ear and whisper, "Every time you end up on the receiving end in prison, I want you to take a look at that scar and remember me. Remember Callie. Remember Sandy. And every other woman you drugged. Whether you got the chance to assault them or not. Remember that we at least had the luxury of being incoherent while you raped us. You won't get that same courtesy in prison, you sorry piece of shit."

I give Josh a couple of quick smacks to his cheek before standing to walk away.

"I'll never go to prison," Josh snorts.

I turn back around and give him my most saccharine grin. "Why do you think I want you to look at the scar, Josh? They have your DNA, dumbass."

Josh smacks his own head on the ground forcing Cal and Brad to lift him up, so he won't hurt himself before the cops get there.

I saunter back over to Callie and Jayden. Throwing my arms over Callie's shoulder I lean into her ear. "Want to go get a hit in real fast? I'm sure no one here will see a thing."

Callie shakes her head. "No way. I can't compete with what you just did. That was so 'badass lead female character' energy! If I went over there now, it would look like the Chihuahua pissing on the same hydrant after the Great Dane. I couldn't meet that bar."

I can't help but snort.

Chapter 28
Brad
One Month Later

Flipping the purple chip over between my fingers, I take a look around the kitchen, watching everyone hustle around to get our Thanksgiving meal ready.

Reed is cutting the ham while James is carving the turkey. Avery is mashing the potatoes. Lola, Chris and her girlfriend, Candace, are slapping the whipped cream on the chocolate and pumpkin pies.

I don't know how long I have been lost in my surroundings when Reed comes over. "Penny for your thoughts?"

I fix my gaze to the chip in my hand. "Just reflecting. Making my list of the people and things I am thankful for."

Reed opens his mouth, about to say something, but the doorbell cuts him off.

I nod toward the group still preparing our dinner. "Go help, I'll get the door."

Reed pats my back and heads back into his large, open kitchen while I walk the opposite direction into his living room. When Reed designed this house, I feel like he did it with family gatherings like this in mind. The kitchen is an entertainer's dream kitchen. Huge island, lots of counter space with wide walkways so two people can pass through, food in hand, without running into each other.

The living room is also very large with an oversized sectional that faces a big bay window. It has a reader's dream seating area in the window and two leather wingback chairs on either side of it that face the couch. Lola's favorite part of the living room is the white curtain that comes down the bay window to create the biggest screen for the projector so that when she watches her cartoons, they take up half the gigantic living room wall.

I drop my chip into my pocket before reaching out to open the front door. I am frozen in place when I see that it is Quinn standing in the doorway, a covered dish in her hands, with Jayden, Cal, and Callie coming up behind her. I step back, opening my arm wide to welcome them all in before leading them into the kitchen.

I could smack Reed right now. Or maybe James. Shit, it could have been Avery that invited them. I want to smack someone. The last thing that I want to do today is sit here and watch Quinn and Jayden cuddling up together.

James' birthday was rough enough. Seeing it today would really test my sobriety.

After I get them all in the kitchen and see that everyone is distracted, I make my way toward the den in the back of the house so I can at least avoid the 'Jayden loves Quinn' show for a few minutes. Give myself time to prepare for it so I don't feel tempted to turn to alcohol. The first week of school was my first real temptation to fall back into old ways. I had to start parking in a different parking spot that was on the other side of the building to avoid walking past Quinn's office every day. I would also get to work thirty minutes earlier than I used to so that I could get my coffee, have my morning chat with Barb, and be out of the lounge before Quinn ever got to work. One time, I was running a little behind, jabbing my jaw too long, but the hum of Quinn's motorcycle lit a fire under me to hightail it back to my classroom.

The second time my sobriety was tested was Halloween night. As if being in the Roost wasn't temptation enough, seeing Quinn there, barely dressed, tested me beyond a point that I thought I would have been able to withstand. When Patsy asked me to be a stand in bouncer for the night, I debated telling her no. Fought with myself for days after telling her that I would, worried that I was setting myself up to relapse.

An hour before I told her I would arrive, I realized that if I stayed home, I would be more tempted to drink because all I could do was think about last Halloween. Sitting at Avery's house with her and Sandy, watching horror flicks after Sandy got home from jail. After seeing Quinn there, I debated telling Patsy that I wasn't ready and leaving. I finally gathered up the courage to do just that when I saw Quinn rip herself out of Josh's arms, throwing herself to the ground. When I found out why, I couldn't help but laugh to myself. My Quinnie brought down the man who not only hurt her, but many other women too. I swear I could hear Sandy celebrating in my mind. When the police took him away, I hit him with the one line that would make both Quinn and Sandy proud…"Have the night you deserve, fucker."

"Oh, shit. Sorry I didn't think anyone else would be in here," Quinn says from behind me.

"Trying to find a quiet place for you and your boyfriend to sneak off to?" I sneer, before turning around to find her standing there alone.

Quinn's eyes go cold. "No. I was scoping out the house for places to hide so I don't have to see you and your girlfriend all but humping at the dinner table tonight," Quinn says, voice rising louder than her normal decibel.

I laugh out, "My girlfriend? If anyone will be humping at the table, it will be you and your boyfriend, just like at your dad's birthday party! You two couldn't even keep your hands off each other when…."

"STOP!" an unfamiliar voice screams.

Quinn and I both whip around to find Lola standing in the doorway.

"Stop fighting!" She screams at us.

Eight pairs of feet can be heard running toward the commotion Quinn and I created and all halt in the hallway when Lola stomps her foot.

"No more fighting!"

Everyone just stands there dumbfounded. It has been a couple of days over the year mark since Lola last spoke, and even then, it was hard to understand half of what she said. But now…here and now, she just spoke perfectly clear.

I can't see where the sniffles in the hallway are coming from, but I can hear them.

Lola points at Quinn and myself. "I have no expensive tears left. You two are in timeout until you can play nicely." With that said, Lola turns on her heel and stomps towards the kitchen, those same eight pairs of feet following her.

I look over at Quinn and see the tears falling down her stunned face. That beautiful, frozen face. I reach over and wipe the tears from the cheek closest to me.

"I am sorry," I whisper.

Her gaze makes its way to me. "Yeah, me too." Quinn exhales a long sigh. "I shouldn't disrespect your relationship. I am sorry. I will not make a scene when she gets here."

I shake my head, completely confused. "Who are you talking about?"

Quinn looks up at me. "Tiffany."

I nearly choke on my laughter. "What the hell are you talking about? Who told you I was dating Tiffany?"

Quinn blushes and looks down at her feet. "I saw her leaving your house."

I run a hand through my hair, racking my mind of any point in time where Tiffany was at my house. It finally hits me. "Wait? You mean the night after your dad's birthday?"

Quinn nods silently.

I laugh again and Quinn narrows her eyes at me.

"Okay, wow. So, yeah, I did sleep with her that night. And please believe me when I say that it is the third biggest mistake of my entire life, but I never dated her, nor have I seen her since that night."

Quinn searches my eyes. "Third?"

"Yeah! Third," I say.

"Then what were the first two?"

I grab Quinn's hands in mine. "The night I stood you up is my first biggest mistake and regret."

Quinn smirks. "Yeah, that one was stupid of you. That still leaves one."

I grip her hands even tighter. "Not telling you that I love you when I had the chance. That's my second biggest mistake and regret."

Quinn pulls her hands out of mine. "I…I'm just…." Quinn points toward the hallway before leaving me behind in the den.

Chapter 29
Quinn

When I step into the kitchen, the site is quite entertaining. Eight adults sitting around, trying to look like they are busying themselves when they all have their eyes glued to the little five-year-old girl rolling the last batch of cookies that need to go in the oven.

I walk up beside Callie, lean my head on her shoulder and whisper, "Did she say anything else?"

Callie gives me a quick glance before whispering back, "Nope. But we are all waiting. Pretty sure everyone has their phone recording right now."

I hear Brad walking up behind me, keeping a safe distance.

"Bunny," I say.

Lola turns around to face me, one eyebrow raised, and one hand on her little hip.

"I wanted to tell you that we are sorry." I step over to Brad and put my arm in his. "We both wanted to tell you that we are sorry." I give him a slight nudge to his rib.

Brad clears his throat. "Yeah, we are both really sorry. We won't be fighting anymore."

Lola's eyes dart between us. "Hug and make up then."

I can't hide the chuckle at the sass in her frass but turn towards Brad, arms open. Brad steps closer, leaning down so that my arms go around his neck, his around my waist. With him leaning down like he is, his face falls into my hair and I can hear him take in a good, long whiff followed by a barely there sigh.

I turn my head slightly to try to whisper in his ear but doing so left us to where our lips are so close together that I can feel his every breath on my lips.

Somewhere in the room, someone clears their throat, giving Brad and I the reality check we needed to pull back from each other. Both of us blushing when we turn back to face Lola.

Like the child is the head of the mafia or something, she waves a hand in the air and says, "I'll accept it," before she turns around and goes back to rolling cookies.

Reed cautiously steps up next to Lola. "Princess…"

Lola sighs and throws the cookie she is rolling down. "Please stop calling me that, Daddy."

Reed is trying vigilantly to hold back his tears. "Do you not like that nickname anymore?"

Lola shakes her head. "A princess is a daughter to a queen. My mother was no queen and killed the one who deserved to be. So, I am not a princess. I am either Queen, or you can find a new name to call me. Lola is acceptable until then."

Avery snorts. "Miss ma'am! When did you go from a five-year-old to a fifteen-year-old? All that sass coming from that cute little…tushy."

Lola smiles at Avery. "I have spent the last year with all of you," Lola says, pointing around the room, "what did you expect?"

The entire room bursts out in laughter, followed by hugs, cheers, tears, and a few sniffles.

"How long have you been talking, Munchkin?" Chris asks Lola.

Lola shrugs. "I have been talking to Dawn for a while. She has been helping me with my words."

Reed lifts Lola up into his arms. "I pay your speech therapist to help you with that…Pumpkin?"

Lola shakes her head. "Please, no. Maybe you should just hire Dawn.

Reed laughs out, "It would save me some money."

I hear a sniffle from behind me and glance over my shoulder to see Brad wiping a tear from his eye. I reach a hand back to grab one of his. He gives my hand a couple of squeezes before he drops it.

"I think it is time to give our thanks and eat. I'm starving," Lola says, clapping her hands together.

Once we have all of the plates and bowls on the table, and everyone has found their spot, Reed stands from the head of the table to lead our round of "thanks."

"I had planned to give thanks to all of you for all you have done for Lola and me this past year, but apparently, I need to change it to giving thanks to Dawn. We will have to invite her over some time so I can properly thank her." Reed looks around the table. "And I am thankful that you are all here with us tonight."

Dad stands to Reed's left. "I am thankful to have us all here tonight. That through tragedy, we have all made our way back here, to each other tonight."

Avery stands up next and peeks down the table to where Candace is sitting. "I promise that we are not normally so gloom and doom. I want to give thanks to our guardian angel that is watching over all of us right now." Avery looks up at the ceiling. "Sandy, I know that you have been beside us all, through the good and the bad, bringing us back together when you saw us drifting apart. Thank you for watching over us…and please don't be mad at me if I totally botched your apple pie recipe. You know I suck with directions."

Chris stifles a giggle and stands up, hugging Avery before Avery sits back down. "I want to give thanks to Avery, for forcing me out of the closet, and throwing me into living my life as a proud lesbian." Chris winks at Candace before continuing, "I did not realize how unhappy I was when I was hiding this part of my life. How weighed down I was. And thank you guys for not making a big deal about it all. Well, except for you Brad, your jokes are awful…but I wouldn't trade them for the world."

Candace goes next. "I want to also give thanks to Avery." Candace reaches over Chris to grab Avery's hand that she extended out to her. "I am glad you outed my girlfriend. You unknowingly fixed the one thing that was holding our relationship back, stunting it in a way. And thank you all for welcoming me into this family."

Brad stands from the other end of the table. "Many years ago, Reed told me that someday I would find someone that I loved so deeply that I would be able to overlook their bad behavior. That I would forgive their lapses in judgement because it came from a place of hurt or vulnerability. I told him that he didn't know me very well if he believed that. Today I want to give thanks to all of you,"

Brad says, looking around the table, pausing on each of us for a few seconds. "Thank you for loving me through my lapses in judgement. Thank you for forgiving me when you did not have to. Thank you for standing beside me through my sobriety."

My head whips to face Brad who is looking directly at me when he says, "I thought that I needed the booze to help me feel numb," Brad stifles a sob before continuing, "but I realize that I was only numbing myself and hurting you in the process. So, thank you all for all the honesty you have all given me. I needed the kick in the ass."

Lola snaps, "Uncle Brad! You said a bad word!"

There are giggles around the table.

Brad nods to Lola. "I am sorry…cutie pie? No, let me try again…cutey patootie? No, no. I can do better than that. I am sorry, peanut."

Lola scrunches her nose and shakes her head.

Brad points at Lola. "I will come up with the perfect one, just give me a few."

Cal stands next. "I want to give thanks to Jayden. I am sorry to say that we all kind of hated you in the beginning…." Everyone but Candace, Callie, and Lola nod at Cal's confession. "But you have proven to us all, on more than one occasion, that we judged you too soon. Thank you for everything you have done, for Sandy, Callie, Flapjack, and every woman that Josh had hurt."

Everyone around the table but Lola starts clapping for Jayden, who gives a single dip of his head.

Cal turns toward Brad. "And I want to thank you for tackling that sorry sack of…"

Reed clears his throat.

Cal glances over at Lola. "That sack of trash…I was going to say trash." Cal looks back at Brad. "I heard everything you said to him while we were waiting, and I want you to know that I am honored to have you as my friend. To know what you would do for the ones you love. Thank you for helping to make sure that my sister, that Flapjack can sleep safely at night now."

Brad reaches over and taps Cal on his arm.

Callie grips Cal's hand after he sits down when she stands. "I want to thank Avery and James for being my first clients this year and helping me get my new business off the ground. Reed, thank you for your help in the financial department. I could never have done this without your investment and help. Chris and Candace, thank you for being my go-to for bakery needs and always helping out with setting up. Brad, thank you for what you did and were willing to do for us. Cal told me. Jayden, thank you for all you have done for all of us. I will keep yours vague because of little ears…" She glances over at Lola and winks at her. Lola responds with her wink blink. "Lola, thank you for gifting us with a true miracle today by getting Brad and Jackie to stop arguing."

Lola giggles.

Callie looks at me. "And Jackie-O. I am so thankful to have *you* back."

A single tear falls down my cheek because I know that she doesn't mean physically. I know that she means the unjaded version of me, and I am thankful to have me back too.

Jayden stands. "I want to give thanks to all of you for taking the time, and chance, to get to know me and welcoming me in with open arms, even after all the misinterpreted situations. I am thankful that the truth has been revealed, and that there is justice for Sandy, Ripper, my cousin, and my girlfriend." Jayden squeezes Callie's hand before sitting down again.

Brad looks at me quizzically and then darts his eyes between Callie and Jayden. Like he doesn't believe what Jayden just said.

I stand up, glancing around at everyone at the table. "I could probably go on for an hour, thanking everyone here but I know that we have a hungry little one over here." I run a hand through Lola's hair. "So, I will make this short and sweet. Thank you all for holding me together when I needed to be held together. For opening your homes to me when mine wasn't available…." I look at Brad. "And for putting me in my place when my britches got too big for me."

Brad gives a slight shake of his head.

Lola jumps up. "I am thankful you guys are done. Now dig in."

Laughter fills the room followed by the sound of everyone filling their plates.

******

Chris, Candace, Avery, Callie, and I are shuffling around the kitchen, cleaning up after dessert. Lola fell into a turkey coma before desserts were even cut. We have been catching up on the bakery, upcoming events that Callie needs our help with, Avery's new business venture which is like a dating service meets pet adoptions, and the plans Chris and Candace have for their Christmas/New Years Eve getaway vacation.

"Can I steal Quinn for a moment?" Brad asks the girls after popping his head into the kitchen.

Of course, they all nod excitedly. Avery even going as far as to push me towards the doorway.

I smack her hands away and then walk toward the back door, motioning for Brad to follow me out there. I imagine we need privacy for this conversation, and I know Avery and Callie are too nosey to give us that privacy.

Once we are outside, Brad leads us over to the wooden swing set off to the right of the yard. "I helped put it together, so, I would trust the swings but not the ladder."

"Duly noted," I say, making my way to one of the swings.

Brad sits in the one beside me. "So, Jayden and Callie?"

I shrug. "They are way better suited than he and I ever were."

"It's not weird or anything?" he asks.

I laugh out, "No way. Callie and I were pogo sisters long before Jayden came into the picture."

Brad raises an eyebrow at me. "Pogo sisters?"

I make bouncing motion. "We shared the same pogo stick...as in we shared the same di…."

Brad puts a hand over my mouth. "Got it, don't need the visual."

I lick his hand to make him pull it away. "You sure? It was at the same time."

Brad contemplates this for a second. "No, I'm sure I don't want the details."

I shrug.

Brad stops his light swaying on the swing. "I am sorry. I truly am."

This time I throw my hand over his mouth. "Enough apologizing. You are forgiven. You have been forgiven for a long time."

Brad bites my palm and I pull my hand back.

"You just bit me!"

Brad lets out a soft laugh before reaching out, grabbing my wrist, pulling my palm to his mouth, and then giving it a light kiss where he had just bitten it.

I am positive he can feel my pulse rate picking up from where his thumb is still on my wrist.

"Brad," I whisper.

"Hmmmm?" he hums out, kissing the heel of my hand that he is still holding.

"We came out here to talk," I say softly.

Brad gives one last kiss to my wrist. "You are right. I have a question for you."

I take a deep breath. "And that is?"

Brad hesitates for a moment before asking, "Do you think we could ever try again?"

I bite my lip to stop myself from blurting out "YES" before giving myself the chance to actually consider it. "I think we could try."

Brad lets out a long exhale. "What would you need that to look like…if we were to try?"

I shrug. "I think if we take it slow, take the time to learn about who we are now compared to who we were a few months ago, that we could see where it goes."

Brad turns his swing to face me, so I turn mine to face him. "Quinn?"

"Yes, Brad?"

"Can I take you on a date Saturday night?"

I let out a soft laugh. "Depends, are you going to show up for this one?"

Brad drops his head.

I grab his cheeks and lift his head up to face me. "I am sorry, I shouldn't joke about that."

Brad grabs both my wrists and kisses the heels of my palms before laying our hands in his lap. "I will show up for this one. I will never leave you hanging ever again."

"Brad…."

Brad shakes his head. "No more. No more talking for tonight." Brad brings my hands to his mouth, kissing both of them again before dropping them. "I will pick you up Saturday at noon. Wear jeans and boots."

I don't say a word as I watch Brad walk back into the house, glancing back at me with a smile every few feet.

Chapter 30
Brad

I am staring at Quinn's front door, hand in the air, ready to knock but I can't bring myself to do it. I have hyped myself up, hoping to hide my nerves but now I don't know if I will be able to do this without fucking it all up. I glance down at the flowers I bought for her, reminding myself that this is our new start. That I need to leave the worries about my previous grievances in the past. I finally get the nerve to knock and thrust my knuckles forward as Quinn opens the door, causing me to bop her on the top of the head when my knuckles didn't have the door to catch them.

Quinn's hand flies to the top of her head and I drop the flowers as I grab both sides of her face, pulling her into me to kiss the spot I just hit.

"Oh my God, I am so sorry! I knew I was going to fuck this up."

Quinn lets out a soft laugh. "It's my fault, I was watching you on my camera for the last five minutes and felt bad for you, so I decided to put you out of your misery. I should have let you suffer a little longer."

I chuckle against her head before kissing it again. "I am so sorry." I lift her head up so she can see my face, to know that I am joking when I say, "but this may have been your karma for getting joy from watching me suffer."

Quinn smacks my hands away with a giggle and then bends down to pick up the flowers I dropped. "These are beautiful."

"Not nearly as beautiful as you are," I say.

Quinn blushes. "I know I said I wanted to take things slow, but we don't have to start at the flattery stage."

"Fine. You look hot."

Quinn laughs. "So, what are we doing on our date?"

"We are going to cut down a Christmas Tree for you. Then, when we get back, we are going to decorate it. Callie picked out the decorations so I imagine you will approve. Oh, and I picked up some hot chocolate with the tiny marshmallows."

Quinn's eyes light up. "What are we standing around talking for then? Let's go!"

******

The tree is decorated, the hot chocolate is gone, I am sitting here on Quinn's couch with her head resting on my lap while we admire the Christmas tree and catch each other up on what life has been like for the last half a year.

I brush my hands through Quinn's hair. "I have really enjoyed today, but it is getting late. I should head home."

Quinn rolls her head over to face me. "Are you sure?"

I nod. "We are going to take it slow…remember."

Quinn bites her bottom lip before responding, "Yeah. You are right."

Quinn rolls off the couch. I stand and stretch, I didn't realize how long we had been sitting there chatting until now. I make my way to the door, Quinn walking behind me.

When I step out onto the porch, I turn around to tell her that I enjoyed myself but can't talk when I see the sad look on her face.

"What is wrong?" I ask.

Quinn shakes her head. "Nothing. I…I just really missed you."

I pull Quinn into a hug, wrapping my arms around her tightly. "God, I missed you too."

Quinn lifts her head to look at me. "Is it too soon for our first kiss?"

I gasp. "Quinnie, are you one of those girls that kisses on the first date?"

The left side of her lip tilts up in a smirk. "You are right, what was I thinking?" She asks, dropping her hands from around my waist, and turning out of my hug.

Without thinking, I grip a hand in her hair, turn her back around to me, and kiss her. Soft at first, but it quickly turns desperate. Not just for me though, I can feel her deepening the kiss too. I don't want to pull away but I know that I need to.

Pulling back, seeing her swollen lips and closed eyes, it is taking more strength to stop myself from leaning back in than it is to hold on to my sobriety.

"Can I take you on another date next Saturday?" I ask her.

Her eyes slowly flutter open and she nods her head. "I would like that."

"I will let you know Friday what time I will pick you up."

Quinn lifts up on her tip toes for another kiss. I bend down to give her a soft, chaste kiss before turning around and heading to my truck. I am proud of myself for enforcing the boundaries Quinn put in place.

Chapter 31
Quinn

Over the last few months, Brad and I have been going on weekly dates, spending the nights we aren't going on dates texting, or going to weekly dinners with the whole group. I have tried to spend more time with him on multiple occasions, but he always declines and goes home after our dates or declines my midweek invite to come over for a movie. I appreciate him taking things slow, but this is a snail's pace that I am beyond tired of.

Avery, Callie, Chris, and I went out shopping for lingerie last weekend. All of us needing something to wear for Valentine's Day. I made sure to stay inside my dressing room when Avery asked for help picking between two sets. I absolutely love her for my dad, but I don't want to even think about the fact that they have sex, or that she dresses in lingerie for him. In my imagination, she buys lingerie for a secret webcam site she has behind my dad's back or some other crazy scenario.

I am adjusting the garter belt back into place when I hear Brad knocking on the front door. I poke my head out of my bedroom door and holler, "It's open."

"Jelly, you shouldn't leave your door unlocked…." Brad starts.

I cut him off. "Take a seat on the couch, I will be out in just a second."

"Okay babe, we need to be out of here in fifteen to make our reservations."

I give myself a mental pep talk and a quick smack to my ass before sauntering into the living room. Clothed only in a deep maroon lace bralette, a matching G-string, and a garter belt connecting to the matching thigh high stockings.

"I think we should cancel the reservation," I say from the hallway.

Brad goes to say something as I enter the living room, but he stops as soon as he sees what I am wearing.

"I can't find shoes to match my outfit…so I think we should just cancel it. What do you think?" I ask, making my way slowly to the couch where he still isn't moving.

"I…Yeah…You…." Brad stutters.

I am standing in front of him now, starting to wonder if I made a huge mistake by pulling this stunt.

Brad finally moves. His hands find the outside of my thighs, and he plays with the top of the stockings. His eyes following the trail his fingers make. He snaps one of the suspenders. "They will figure it out when we don't show."

His eyes trail up my body, slowly taking in what I am wearing. Appreciation glittering in his eyes. "Are you sure?" he asks when his eyes finally make it up to mine.

I nod my head. "Yes," I breathe out.

Brad lightly pushes me back so that he can stand from the couch. His hands push my hair back behind my shoulders before he walks around me. "You look magnificent. From every angle."

I stand still in front of him. Waiting.

"Do you have condoms?"

I shake my head. "I forgot to grab any and haven't had a need for any for a long time. I got checked last month and I am clean. I am still on birth control, too."

His hand trails up my stomach, between my breasts, and stops when he gets to my neck. Gripping under my jaw lightly, he pulls me into him. "I tested clean in August and haven't been with anyone since. Are you sure this is what you want?"

I nod. "I am sure."

His grip around my neck tightens just enough to build anticipation. "Thank God," he growls before crashing his mouth on mine.

I grasp for his clothing, wanting to rip it off as quickly as possible. He drops his hand from my neck to help me undress him. When the last of his clothes hit the floor, he leans down, picks me up, my legs wrapping around his waist, as he carries me to my room.

His hands digging into the flesh between my thong and stockings. "Fuck, I need you," he gasps out.

Between kisses on his chest I say, "Me too, Pookie. Me too."

Brad kicks my door open, slamming me into it so he can use the door to help hold me up while his hands travel up my body. "I may not last long."

I gasp from the feel of him pinching my nipples through the lace. "We have all night for more."

One of Brad's hands go to the back of my neck, the other around my ass as he moves us from the door to the bed. He throws me down on it and lightly smacks the inside of my knees. "Spread 'em. Let me see what's mine."

I spread my legs so he can see what truly is his. He runs a finger around the tiny triangle that barely covers my slit, pulling a dripping wet finger away. He gives one side of his finger that is covered in my juices a lick before holding it in front of my mouth. I suck the finger in, rolling my tongue around it, and then pull my head back to pop it out of my mouth.

"I missed that mouth of yours, too. We will have to save that for later though," Brad says before dropping down between my knees and licking me through the lace.

My fingers grip his hair, pulling him harder into me. "I need you in me. Now."

Brad pulls his head up. "I want to…."

"We have time for that later. Fuck me. Now."

Brad runs his hands up the outside of my thighs, grabs the tiny strings on my thong and rips it in half.

"Yes! This is what I'm talking about," I say, shimmying down to where he is kneeling.

Brad grips my hips and flips me over onto my stomach. I arch my back, pushing my ass higher up in the air, my right cheek flat on the bed. Brad runs his cock through my slit, lubing it up with my dripping juices before smacking the head of his dick against my clit.

Sliding his dick in me, his murmured curses build me up higher. "Fuck, Jelly. You are so damn tight."

I push back against him harder, enjoying the slight sting as we rush to get him fully inside me. It takes a few more thrusts on both of our ends to finally get there. Once he is fully in me, though, we give ourselves a couple of seconds to acclimate. His balls are resting against my clit, keeping a steady pressure there until he starts pumping into me. The slapping against my clit sends me falling into my first orgasm before we even have a chance to break a sweat.

"Jelly, God, you are squeezing me so tight," Brad breathes out, hands gripping my ass so hard that he is breaking skin.

Brad picks up his pace, creating a symphony of our moans, grunts, and bodies slapping together. One of his hands slides up my back and wraps around my hair, pulling my head off the bed. He is pounding into me so hard that my ass cheeks and pussy are already tender. Each sting on my sensitive skin is getting me closer to my next orgasm.

I can tell he is getting close, too. His strokes are becoming less rhythmic and more frantic. I reach between my legs so that I can rub against his balls with each thrust. He lets go of my ass and moves that hand around to my clit. This was all I needed. My orgasm racks me so hard, I fall forward, Brad releasing inside me at the same time with a low groan before he falls on top of me.

He gives himself a few seconds to catch his breath before he rolls over onto his back. I curl into his side, draping a leg over his waist as he lazily strokes my leg.

"I missed this, Pooks."

"Me, too, Jelly. Me, too."

Epilogue
Reed

"Let's see, where did we leave off? So, I told you how Brad and Jack finally figured their stuff out. The last time we talked, I told you how they were going on their first date again. He did finally tell me the story about how they met. It all happened over a rigged bet. He didn't know it was rigged when he took the bet. He definitely found his match with her. He is planning to propose tonight at dinner. She is going to hate it because she is like you when it comes to having everyone's attention on her.

Avery and James have decided they are going to get married. I am sure she has already told you about that. Or maybe Lola did. I swear since that girl has started talking again, she doesn't stop. It's the best. It's going to be a small wedding, and Lola is the only one in it. Avery said she wouldn't have bridesmaids or groomsmen because then she wouldn't have anyone to watch them get married. You know, our family has grown a little in the past two years.

Jayden and Callie are doing well; they are moving to the big city soon. Between his construction business and her party planning business, they were driving out there so much, it just made sense for them to move out that way. Lola is excited to have a place closer to all the theme parks to stay at that isn't a hotel.

Chris and Candace are thriving. I bet we will have another wedding there coming up in the near future. They are making the wedding cake for Avery and James. Oh, and Callie will be planning that, of course.

Cal has started seeing someone, he hasn't told any of us much about him yet, it is pretty new, but Callie swears we will all like him. I am sure we will.

Lola and Memaw are baking tonight. She wants to learn how to make all of your goodies so that she can work for Candace when she is old enough. I swear that girl is too mature for her age, already planning her life goals.

I guess that leaves me…I still haven't sold the house. I took down the signs, told the realtor to hold off on showing it. I sneak over there still when I am alone. I sit in the office, in our bedroom, and I swear it is almost like I can replay all the good times we had in my mind. Almost like I can watch a movie of us if I just close my eyes and think about you. It is silly, but sometimes, I feel like you are back there with me, like I can smell your lotion, or feel a small gust of wind, like you walked past me.

I know I need to get rid of it, but I just can't bring myself to do it yet. Maybe the next time I come to talk to you, I will be strong enough to do it.

Charles's trial is coming up for his involvement in everything. I will keep you updated about that. Josh is serving a minimum of twenty-five years for everything he has done. He should be thankful. I finally found out what Brad said to him while waiting for the cops to get him. Brad openly told him that if the cops ever let him walk out of that jail, that Brad would be waiting for him and would make sure he never left the parking lot alive. Told him that he had nothing to live for, so why not take out the trash and kill two birds with one stone."

I run a hand over Sandy's head stone and reposition the flowers.

"I have rambled on enough. I need to get back to Memaw's. We are doing our first annual Thanksmas tomorrow. Lola's idea of course. She said we needed a happy reason to come out here so that Memaw wouldn't be sad every time we came and left. I love you and miss you, Baby. Until I see you again, keep watching over us."

Acknowledgements

I have to start my acknowledgements off with a big THANK YOU to my editor, Adi, again. Thank you for not only helping me build these stories into what they are, but also for being my sounding board through everything! You are my most favorite editor I have ever had. I mean, you are the only one I have ever had but you set a high bar. I love you so much!

Author Jessie Called, thank you for being my other solid rock through all three books! I can never repay you for all the guidance you have given me! I am truly blessed to have you as a friend and a colleague!

Nurse "K", thank you for being my go-to for questions regarding Quinn's work. I appreciate you patiently putting up with my off the wall questions!

About The Author

Jannah is a stay-at-home mom who spends most days catering to little humans and her fur doggies. When she is not busy with housework, kids, or her geriatric dogs, she is writing, reading, or listening to books.

The only time she watches TV is during hockey season. GO CAPS!

If there were an award for being Murphy's Law Number One Target, she would own it.

Her favorite hobby is baking mass quantities of cookies to disperse to her physical therapists, tanning gals, and anyone else she feels needs a cookie hug at the time.

Want to keep up with the author, Brad, see what is next to come, or watch Jannah's Murphy's Law chronicles? Follow her on any of these socials.

Facebook: Author Jannah Jette
Instagram: @authorjannahjette
Tiktok: @author.jannah.jette
Email: jannahjettesocials@gmail.com

Want to see the Turtle painting Avery bought James? Check out Melissa Williams art at ViaMeliaArt.com. Sandy and James won't be the only one in this series who receives one of Melissa's paintings. Be on the lookout for the final book in The Three Shots Series, For Those Who Need Help To Feel to see what Brad buys!

Books In This Series The Three Shots Series

The Three Shots Series follows a group of friends turned family as they navigate through healing from their past and present trauma while finding love and loss along the way.

For Those Who Hurt- Sandy leaves her hometown after finding her boyfriend having an affair with his secretary. She is heading East to room with her best friend and is ready to start her new and improved life. Should she have stayed in her hometown?

For Those Who Heal- Avery found a lucrative way to kill two birds with one stone. One client flips Avery's life upside down and takes her on an emotional rollercoaster, forcing her to face past demons. Will she come out of this healed or brokenhearted?

For Those Who Need Help to Feel- Brad is struggling to keep up the facade that he is okay until a woman comes along who makes him feel again. Can he put aside his coping crutch in time to keep her, or is history doomed to repeat itself?

www.ingramcontent.com/pod-product-compliance
Lightning Source LLC
LaVergne TN
LVHW100514110826
845146LV00002B/640
* 9 7 9 8 9 9 9 8 1 0 4 7 2 *